USBORNE
Forgotten Fairy Tales
of BRAVE AND
Brilliant GIRLS

Retold by Susanna Davidson, Rosie Dickins,
Andy Prentice and Rob Lloyd Jones,
with a foreword by Kate Pankhurst

Illustrated by Isabella Grott,
Alessandra Santelli and Maria Surducan

Contents

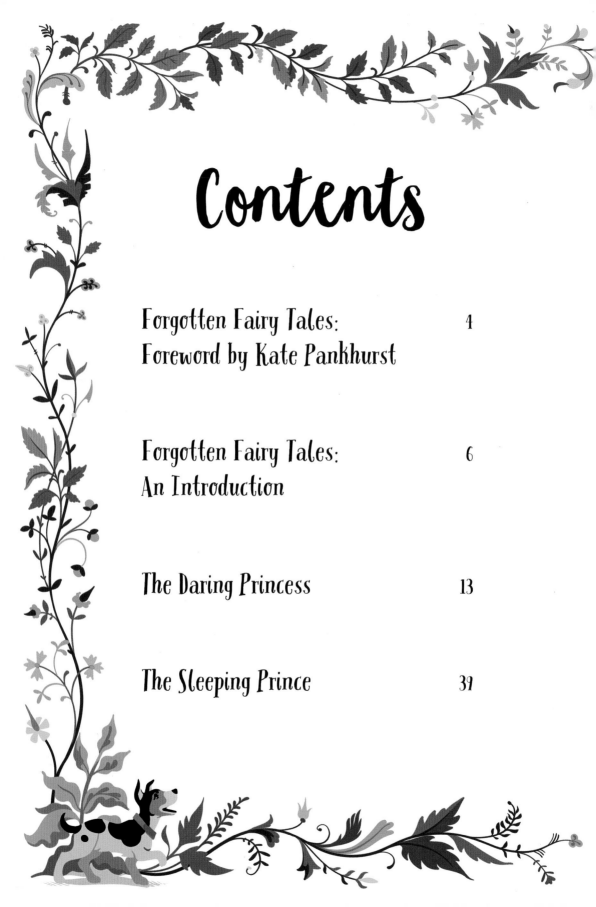

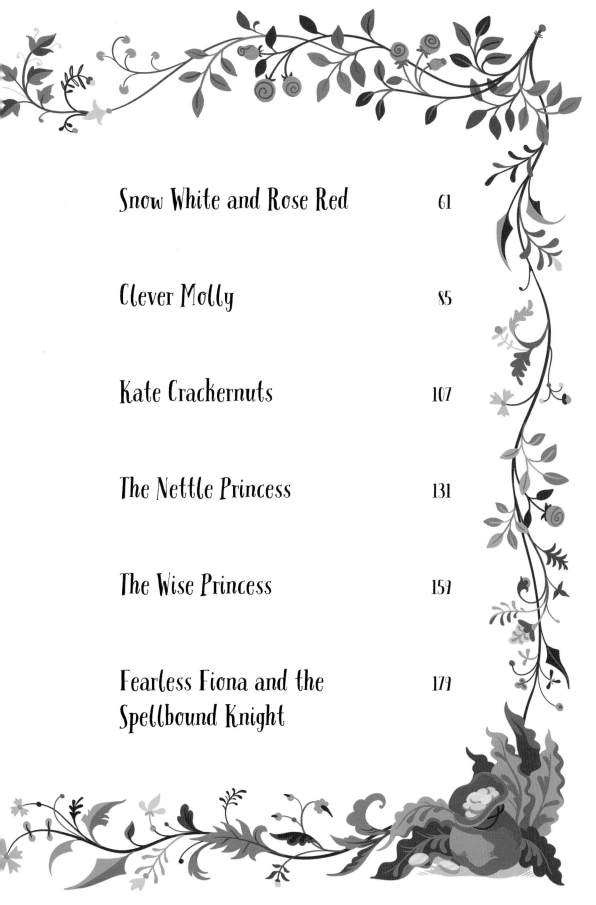

Forgotten Fairy Tales

Foreword

I firmly believe that stories have magical powers. (How fitting with a fairy tale does that sound? But it's definitely true!) Stories can enchant our imaginations and shape our view of the world; they can even make us think differently about ourselves. That's why this book, bursting with brave and brilliant heroines, telling us stories almost lost to history, is so exciting and

so very different to the versions of the fairy tales available when I was young.

If I think back, the girls I read about in fairy stories did spend a LOT of time hanging around in towers, waiting to be rescued. They also spent much of the story in a bewitched sleep, waiting for a prince to arrive. The stories you are about to read are different: the actions of our heroines better reflect the world we live in, who you are, and who I know you will become.

I hope that they inspire you to be brave and brilliant, and to question anyone who says you are anything else. Your story is yet to be written, but I know it won't be forgotten...

Kate Pankhurst

Forgotten Fairy Tales

An Introduction

F or thousands of years, people have been telling fairy tales to each other:
on sunny days, to while away the time,
or on long, dark evenings around the fire.
These tales were remembered and passed
on, from friend to friend, from parents
to children, across borders and over
time. All the stories shared one common
thread – like living things, they were
always changing, as they danced from one
storyteller to the next.

Then, a few hundred years ago, the old,
wild stories began to be hunted and tamed.
Collectors came. They gathered up the
stories they heard, and set about writing
them down, trapping them between the
pages of their books.

Now, in some ways, this was a very fine thing. The great story-hunters – such as the Brothers Grimm in Germany, or Andrew and Nora Lang in Scotland – gave everyone a gigantic gift by keeping the old tales alive. Even today, they continue to light up our lives. The most famous have become the most often-told stories in the world – the stories that everyone listens to at bedtime or watches on a screen.

But something was lost when the stories were written down. The collectors cooked up their own versions. It's true that a fairy tale should be told the way you want, but it does mean that many of our most famous stories had the ideas – and ideals – of the time baked into them, and they are still being told that way today.

Many of these ideas we now consider very old-fashioned. Women were often shown as weaker than men. There were more princesses waiting to be rescued than there were brave heroines who saved the day. This is true for some of our most famous fairy tales – *Cinderella, Snow White* and *Sleeping Beauty.*

As these tales became famous, they overshadowed all the others. There could be room for only one princess in a tower. *Rapunzel* loomed over *The Nettle Princess* like a skyscraper over a gingerbread cottage. The brave and brilliant girls were hidden from view.

Stories die when they are not told, and we want to bring some of the forgotten fairy tales back to life.

Why is it so important that these tales are not forgotten? Because fairy tales fire our imaginations, and they can shape our understanding and our expectations for our lives. A fairy tale that stays with you can make you see the world in a whole new way.

The eight forgotten fairy tales in this book are bursting with brave, daring women, who rescue princes, go on adventures, fight with giants and climb impossible mountains.

Some of the tales are less forgotten than others, but even if you think you know them, you may find they have changed shape. Like all storytellers, we have told them in the way we thought best. And, if you really love a fairy tale,

you can retell it too. If you want, you can change endings and meanings in the way *you* think best. Who knows, your story may in turn be told and told again. So enjoy these adventures and then tell them to your friends...

This fairy tale is based on a story called 'The Iron Stove' which was retold by the Brothers Grimm.

The Daring Princess

There are princesses, and then there are *princesses*. The *princesses* swan around in palaces making gowns out of silk and gossamer. Or they sit in towers and sing to bluebirds, while dreaming of being rescued.

Bessie knew she definitely didn't want to be *that* kind of princess.

The other kind of 'princess' is much more ordinary. These princesses have royal parents and live in palaces and sew and sing (but not to bluebirds). They are very polite and good and always have spotlessly clean clothes. Bessie knew she didn't want to be *that* kind of princess either.

Bessie was happiest in the stables, grooming her old pony, or chatting to the royal blacksmith, watching him at work. Over her skirts she kept a tool belt. She knew how to pick a lock, make a horseshoe and even forge a sword.

But Bessie's parents were increasingly unhappy that their daughter was turning out to be such an unusual princess. Just that morning, her mother had asked when she was going "to start learning to sew?" and her father had complained that she wasn't behaving "as a princess should."

"And don't think we approve of your tool belt," added her mother. "It's not ladylike. And it's *definitely* not princess-like."

Then her parents had sighed and looked disappointed and muttered things about "duty" and "changing her ways."

Bessie had a horrible feeling that her days of gallivanting around the castle grounds were numbered. Soon, her parents were going to make her start sewing and singing and ban her visits to the blacksmith. That thought had made her want to get as far away from the castle as possible. She had fled to the royal forest... and now she was lost.

Bessie looked around, hoping to find a tree or a path she recognized, but she had never been so deep in the forest before and she had no idea where she was. And all the time, the sky grew darker and she tried very hard not to think of prowling wolves and what might lie hidden in the shadows.

At last, after hours of wandering, she came across a tiny wooden cottage, with a thatched roof and a little crooked chimney.

"With luck," Bessie thought, "whoever lives here can help me get home."

She knocked three times but there was no
answer, only a strange muffled sound, like a voice
calling from far away.

"Hello?" Bessie said,
and the muffled sound
came again.

She lifted the latch
and the door swung open.
The cottage had just one
room, and it appeared to
be empty. There was a
wooden chair in the
corner, a faded rug on
the floor, and bunches

of dried herbs hanging from the ceiling. On the
worktop she could see a pestle and mortar for
grinding, and shelves lined with glass bottles,
which glowed green and purple and amber. In the
middle of the room was a very large and rather
rusty iron stove.

"Help," said a voice from inside the stove.

"I'm trapped in here. Please! Let me out!"

Bessie darted forward, and then stopped. She looked again at the glowing glass bottles and saw they were full of curious things, like frogs' legs, eyeballs and a green snake, twisted and coiled.

"I must be in a witch's cottage!" cried Bessie.

"You are," came the muffled voice from the stove.

"Then how do I know you're not an evil spirit? Or a gremlin? Or a troll?" asked Bessie.

"I'm not. I'm a prince," said the voice. "Prince Alfred. There's a tiny crack halfway down. You can see for yourself."

Bessie bent down and peered through the crack. "Goodness!" she cried. For there, inside the stove, was a rather squished-looking young man.

"Definitely not a gremlin or a troll," thought Bessie. "You poor thing!" she said out loud. "Don't worry. I'll get you out!"

She took a knife from her tool belt and began to scrape away at the iron stove until there was a small hole.

"Hurry," said Prince Alfred. "Please hurry! The witch may be back at any moment!"

Bessie kept going, even though her fingers were sore and her arms ached, until the hole was big enough for the prince to reach out his arm... and then a leg...

"Only a little more," pleaded the prince.

Bessie worked as the night drew in and the moon came out, until at last, the prince stood free.

"Thank you for rescuing me," he said. "I owe

you my life. A witch has trapped me here – until our wedding day. She said only a princess could save me."

"Well she was right," said Bessie, returning her knife to her tool belt. "I am a princess."

"You're quite an *unusual* princess," said Prince Alfred, staring at the belt. "I've never met a princess before who carries tools with her."

Bessie sighed. "You sound just like my parents. They don't think being unusual is a good thing for a princess. They want me to learn to sing beautifully and make cushion covers."

But Prince Alfred was smiling. "Only an unusual princess could have saved me," he said. "I'm very grateful it was *you* who found me. No amount of sewing would have freed me from this stove."

The prince opened his mouth, as if he were about to speak again, but at that moment the cottage door swept open. A foul-smelling green wind howled its way into the little room. When it cleared, there stood a woman in a long black cloak,

with flowing hair. She had yellow
fingernails as sharp as knives
and glaring eyes, one green,
one blue. Bessie knew her
at once for the witch.

"Did you think you
could escape me so easily?"
she snarled, striding
towards the prince.

There was a great clap,
like thunder, and a flash of
light. When Bessie looked again,
both the witch and Prince Alfred had vanished.

Stumbling out of the cottage, all she could see
were the dark shapes of the trees. "I must find
the prince," she vowed. "Perhaps if I climb a tree,
I'll be able to see where he's gone."

A great oak tree grew beside the cottage, with
branches low enough for her to climb.

Bessie clambered from branch to branch until
she was peeking out, over the treetops. There was

no sign of the prince, but she did see a light, twinkling between the trees, not far off.

"I'll follow the light," she decided. "Perhaps it will lead me to someone who can help..."

So Bessie climbed down from the tree and felt her way through the darkness, towards the light.

At last she came to a little house with grass growing all around and a pile of wood by the small front door. Bessie bent down and peered through the window. Inside, she could see a group of toads. Some were big, some little, and they were sitting at a beautifully laid table, with one little toad on the floor. There was a white tablecloth, a dish of roasted meats and silver cups.

Bessie knocked loudly and heard the largest toad call out:

Little green toad,
Get up from the floor!
Pull back the lock and open the door.

At once, the door opened and Bessie stepped inside. The toads all rushed to welcome her.

"Please, sit down," said the largest toad. "What are you doing so deep in the woods, so late at night?"

Bessie told them her story, about the prince and the iron stove and how the witch had come and whisked him away. "Now I don't know where the prince has gone or how I shall ever find him," she finished.

"Well now," said the largest toad, "you have come to the right place, for we are able to help you. But first, you must rest."

Bessie was given food and then taken to a beautifully made bed with silken covers, woven with gold and silver thread. When the next day was dawning, the large toad turned to the little toad again and said:

Little green toad, now try your best.
Get down from the table and open the chest.

The little green toad did just as the big toad asked and threw open a chest that stood in the corner. Out of it, the large toad took six enormous darning needles, a cartwheel and three nuts.

"You will need to cross an ice mountain, a field of slashing swords and a great lake. When you have passed these, you will find the prince again. Take these objects. You can use them to help you on your journey."

Bessie thanked the toads and left with the first light of day.

It wasn't long before she came to a towering mountain made of gleaming ice. Bessie tried to climb it, but it was so steep, and so slippery, that no sooner had she taken a few steps than she slid down again. "I've failed already!" she thought. "I'll never rescue the poor prince."

Then she remembered the needles the toads had given her. She pushed three into the side of the mountain, placed her foot on them and began to climb.

With each step, she had to pierce the ice with the needles and then pluck them out again. The needles were so sharp they slid in easily, but it was slow work and the sun was already setting by the time she reached the very top.

"At least getting down will be quicker," thought
Bessie. And, with a whoop, she slid all the way
down the other side.

Bessie camped in a glade that night, for it was
too dark to go on. But when morning broke, she
saw that beyond her lay the field of slashing swords.

The field sloped downwards, stretching
endlessly towards the horizon. The swords were
closely packed and whirled over the ground, round
and round, as if powered by invisible hands. Their
blades flashed and dazzled in the sun and Bessie
knew there was no way she could walk across and
come out unharmed. Then she remembered the
cartwheel the toads had given her...

Plucking up her courage, Bessie balanced on
the wheel, arms outstretched, and rolled it through
the sword-filled field. It took her all day. By the
time she reached the other side she knew it was
too dark to go on. This time, she lay down to rest
on a sandy beach, and went to sleep to the sound of
waves, lapping against the shore.

The Daring Princess

Plucking up her courage, Bessie balanced on the wheel, arms outstretched, and rolled it through the sword-filled field.

The next morning, by the light of dawn, Bessie saw that she was at the edge of a great lake, which seemed as deep and wide as the sea. Not knowing what else to do, she cracked open the first nut. Inside was a tiny boat, no bigger than a pea. She placed it on the water where it grew and grew, until it was large enough for Bessie to climb inside.

She sailed across the lake and landed on the far shore, in the shadow of a magnificent castle.

Night was drawing in, but in one of the tower windows a light flickered. Stepping closer, Bessie saw the witch, silhouetted against the window. She saw her long flowing hair and her long yellow fingernails. The witch was gazing at herself in a mirror and laughing.

Bessie saw her reach for a small glass bottle. The witch gulped down the liquid inside and a moment later she was transformed into a beautiful young woman. With a smile, she placed a dazzling crown on her head.

"If the witch is here, then maybe the prince is

here too," thought Bessie. "I have to find him."

Taking a deep breath, Bessie pushed open the great front door and crept into the castle.

There was a huge hall and a sweeping staircase, and to her left and right, long, narrow corridors that seemed to go on forever. The castle was filled with servants, hurrying back and forth, carrying dishes piled high with food.

"Excuse me," said Bessie, stopping one of the servants. "Why are you all rushing so?"

The servant looked at her, surprised. "We're preparing for the wedding, of course," he said. "The princess is marrying Prince Alfred tonight."

"And where is the prince?" asked Bessie.

The servant looked around, as if to make sure no one could hear him, then he bent down to whisper in Bessie's ear. "He's sleeping in the topmost tower," he said. "He's been sleeping ever since he got here... almost as if he's under a spell. The princess visits him each night, bringing him one of her potions."

The Daring Princess

"How would I find my way to the tower?" asked Bessie.

"At the end of this corridor is a turret staircase. Keep climbing till you reach the very top," the servant whispered, and then he hurried away.

Bessie walked the great length of the corridor. When she reached the foot of the staircase, she plucked a candle from the wall and began to climb. Up and up and up she went, as if climbing to the clouds. The turret seemed to be getting narrower all the time, the stairs almost twisting back on themselves, but at last she reached a little door, right at the very top. Bessie pushed open the door and there, on a narrow bed, the prince lay sleeping.

Bessie called out to try and wake him, but he didn't stir. She shook him, once, twice, three times, but still the prince slept on.

"You have to wake up!" cried Bessie. "Please! Wake up! The witch is here and she's going to make you marry her."

Nothing that Bessie did would wake him.

Then she remembered her gifts from the toads; she still had two nuts left. Bessie cracked one open and saw that inside was a thick golden liquid. She held the nut to Prince Alfred's lips and let the liquid drip between them.

After one drop, the prince's breathing quickened. After another, his eyes fluttered open and as the third passed his lips, he sat up and looked at Bessie.

"You came!" he said.

"I did," replied Bessie. "Even though I had to climb an ice mountain, pass through a field of slashing swords and cross a lake to reach you."

"You are the bravest princess I know," said Prince Alfred. "You have saved me again."

"We aren't safe yet," Bessie replied. "I saw the witch through the castle window. She drank a potion and transformed herself into a beautiful young woman."

"I know," said the prince. "She works all day in her tower, stirring up magic and perfecting her horrible potions. Then she comes to me each night at nine, just as I wake, and makes me drink her potions again."

Even as he spoke, the castle clock began to chime.

Ding! Ding! Ding! Ding! Ding! Ding! Ding! Ding!

Ding! Ding!

"Then what are we waiting for!" said Bessie.

Hand in hand, they rushed down the stairs and out of the castle door. There was the boat, waiting for them. Together, they sailed across the great lake, and together, they crossed the field of swords and climbed the ice mountain.

"We're not far now from my parents' castle," said Bessie. "It's just on the other side of this forest."

But behind them came a howling green wind, and on the wind they heard a cackling cry.

"The witch!" shouted Prince Alfred. "She's coming for us. We'll never outrun her."

"It was all for nothing," thought Bessie, until she remembered she still had one gift left from the toads. She reached into her pocket, pulled out the last nut, and cracked it open.

Out sprang a white stallion, pawing the ground and tossing its mane.

Bessie and the prince leaped onto its back and galloped through the forest. The green wind raged after them, but it was no match for the stallion.

They heard the roar of the wind weaken, until it was no more than a whisper, fluttering through the leaves.

At last, they reached the castle gates. Bessie pulled up the stallion, its flanks heaving, while her parents came rushing out of the castle to greet them.

"You've come back to us," cried Bessie's father. "We thought we'd lost you forever."

When Bessie and the prince told their story, Bessie's parents beamed with pride.

"And where is your home?" Bessie's mother asked the prince.

Prince Alfred shook his head sadly. "My home is on the other side of the ice mountain. Soon after my parents died, the witch came to our castle and claimed it as her own. She cast a spell on my brothers and sisters. I don't know what happened to them or where they went. She locked me in an iron stove, saying I had to stay there until I was ready to marry her."

"We'll keep you safe from the witch now," said Bessie. "And together, we can search for your brothers and sisters."

They didn't have to look far. The next day, the king and queen threw a party to celebrate Bessie's return. Everyone in the kingdom was invited.

One family looked strangely familiar. They all smiled at Bessie and shook her hand. But when they saw the prince, they rushed into his arms.

"My brothers and sisters!" cried Prince Alfred. "Where have you been?"

"The witch turned us all into toads," said the eldest sister. She looked at Bessie. "When you freed our brother from the castle and brought him to your home, you broke her spell. You were brave and strong and true."

"Three cheers for the daring princess!" cried the king. "The very best kind of princess of all."

Everyone raised their glasses and cheered, "To the daring princess. Hip hip hooray!"

The king and queen never again suggested
Bessie should be better behaved. She was allowed
to roam the forests and forge her swords and
ride her fine white stallion. She became famous
throughout the land for her courage, and after
her parents' death, she ruled the kingdom wisely
and well.

As for the witch – she was never seen again.
The cottage in the forest stayed empty and no
howling green wind returned to haunt the castle.
Bessie often wondered what had happened to
her, and what she was doing now with her
powerful magic.

Prince Alfred, his brothers and sisters all
returned home, but the younger children said they
missed their life as toads. When they were old
enough, they went back to live in their little house,
to offer a refuge for those lost in the woods.

Bessie never forgot the prince. Whenever she
had the time, she would scale the ice mountain and
cross the field of slashing swords and the great lake

to see him, and they remained the very truest and best of friends.

"I will always be grateful to you," said Prince Alfred, on one of her visits.

"And I to you," Bessie replied. "For you opened up my life to adventure..."

This fairy tale is based on an old Spanish story 'El rey durmiente en su lecho' which means 'The Prince Sleeping in his Bed'.

The Sleeping Prince

*L*ong, long ago, there was a princess who was very, very bored. As the daughter of the king and queen, she wasn't allowed to go fishing for sharks, or climb tall trees, or even get her dress crumpled. Instead, she just had to sit and watch everyone from her balcony.

To keep cheerful, the princess liked to imagine herself going on thrilling adventures in faraway places. She sent herself to jungle-choked islands packed with mysterious temples. She trekked across icy wastes in search of a dragon's treasure. In time, she became an excellent storyteller – although no one else ever heard her stories.

One day, she was up in her usual spot, lost in one of her daydreams, when she heard a sweet song. Down below her, some children were skipping with a rope and singing:

The prince he sleeps and does not wake
Until midsummer evening.

The princess was curious. She had never heard this song before.

"What is that song you are singing?" she called down to them.

"Um… it's from a bedtime story my mother told me, Your Majesty," replied one of the girls, a little nervously.

"Tell it to me," ordered the princess.

"My mother says that in a faraway castle, a bewitched prince passes the whole year asleep. He only wakes up for one hour on the evening of the Midsummer festival. Then he falls asleep again until the following year. They say he will remain this way, until he wakes to find a princess at his bedside."

"I'm a princess," thought the princess. "I could save him."

"How far away is this castle?" she asked, trying to keep the eagerness out of her voice.

"I don't know, but my mother said that to arrive there you would have to..." the girl hesitated, "...break some iron boots?" She shrugged.

"That always sounded rather crazy to me."

The princess wasn't daunted by these strange directions. That very day she ordered the palace cobbler to craft a pair of iron boots in her size. She asked that they be hard-wearing, but stylish. The cobbler set to work at once. As soon as the boots were finished, the princess crept out of the castle and put them on. She clumped and clanked towards the setting sun. Even though she was wearing three pairs of socks, her new boots were heavy and chafed terribly. Soon her feet were covered in blisters.

But the princess did not stop, not even when she came to a magic forest that no man dared to enter.

"It's lucky I'm not a man," said the princess, when a goatherd tried to warn her about the forest's dangers.

After walking some time, she came to a fragrant flower-filled clearing. A friendly old lady was picking herbs nearby.

"Where are you heading?" asked the lady.

"I'm going in search of the sleeping prince who never wakes except on Midsummer evening," the princess replied. "Do you happen to know where his castle is?"

"I've no idea, I'm afraid." The old lady shook her head. "But my son, the Sun, might know."

"The Sun?" said the princess, a little alarmed.

"Yes, yes, the actual Sun." The old lady sounded impatient, as if she'd had to explain this before. "He's a very bright lad but also very grumpy. And there's a problem. You see, he likes to eat people."

The princess was as brave as she was determined. She insisted on going back to the old lady's house, despite the danger. Before the Sun arrived home, she hid herself inside a rather dusty wardrobe.

Peering through the keyhole, she watched the Sun arrive. He was a giant, and he shone so brightly that it was impossible to see his face. His clothes almost seemed to be on fire.

Suddenly, the Sun cried out and began to take great snorting sniffs through his nose.

"I smell human flesh!" he shouted, blazing with light. "I want to eat it!"

"Simmer down, you silly boy," said the old lady. "I want to ask you a question. In the forest I met a young girl. She's looking for the castle of the prince who's always asleep. Do you know where it is?"

"I've never heard of it or him!" roared the Sun. "No doubt my sisters, the Stars, might have an idea. Ask them."

With that, he gave an enormous yawn and strode off to bed.

Exhausted by her journey, the princess fell asleep too, right there, in her wardrobe. She dreamed deep until her ravenous hunger and a savage crick in her neck woke her up just before dawn.

Soon the Sun went out to start the morning. The old lady prepared the princess a delicious breakfast of fresh eggs and porridge. She gobbled it up as the Star sisters returned, one by one, from a long night's twinkling. They were very tired too.

One by one, the princess asked them her question, but none of the Stars had heard of the sleeping prince or his castle.

"Maybe the Wind would be the one to ask," chimed the last of the Stars. "He's always rushing everywhere, getting into every nook and cranny, and he's always on the move. I'm sure, if anyone knows, he would."

Carrying a small picnic that the old lady insisted she take, the princess set out once again in her iron boots. She clumped along through the ancient forest, passing beneath mighty trees whose topmost, moss-encrusted branches soared higher than cathedrals. Strange flowers glittered in the shadows and strange birds twittered from the bushes. The princess refused to be distracted by these incredible sights. Grimly ignoring her blisters, she clanked on.

"How long will it take me to wear out these boots?" she wondered. "They seem very sturdy."

The princess ate her lunch on a sun-dappled

rock that overlooked a murmuring stream. Shortly after, she met another old woman.

"Where are you headed in such stylish iron boots?" asked the old woman.

"I'm going in search of the sleeping prince, who never wakes except on Midsummer evening," the princess replied. "Do you happen to know where his castle is?"

The old woman thought for a moment. "No, I don't know the place. But maybe my son, the Wind, will have some idea. Only I'm afraid that he'll blow you away if he sees you. He's very grumpy... and he also likes to eat people," she added, as an afterthought.

The princess was as determined as she was practical. Naturally, she insisted on going back to the old lady's house. Before the Wind arrived home, she once again hid herself in a wardrobe. But, this time, she remembered to take a pillow in with her, so it was more comfortable than before.

Peering through a crack in the door, she watched as the Wind burst in, with a roar.

"I smell human flesh!" he bellowed, sniffing and snuffling at the air. "I want to eat it."

"Pipe down, you silly boy," said the old lady. "And answer this question. In the forest I met a nice girl with a fantastic eye for footwear. She was looking for the castle of the prince who is always asleep. Do you know where it is?"

"Hah! That's easy," hooted the Wind. "She simply has to go out of this house by the back door, and keep walking. She'll find it if she wants it enough. Now, where's my dinner?"

The old lady served him a chilled pear soup, a whole wheel of cheese and a cauldron of gooseberries. The Wind sucked it all down with great gusto.

Sitting comfortably in her wardrobe, the princess patiently waited for the Wind to leave, which soon he did.

Thanking his mother, she followed the Wind's instructions and left the house by the back door. After clumping for some way, she came to a towering thicket of thorns. The spines were as long and sharp as carving knives.

"I won't go back," muttered the princess, fiercely. "So, onwards!"

The princess was as practical as she was clever. She waded straight into the thicket, crushing the thorns with her trusty iron boots. She made quick progress but was surprised suddenly to feel the soft crumble of bare earth through her socks.

Looking down, she realized that her iron boots had completely worn away on the savage thorns. Looking up again, she saw a magnificent castle.

A magnificent castle... had appeared out of nowhere,
right in front of her...

It had appeared out of nowhere, right in front of her, and all the thorns had vanished away. Beyond it, the ocean sparkled. Waves crashed on the cliffs far below. The castle's wide doors gaped open, invitingly.

The princess padded inside in her socks. She found the castle richly furnished but almost empty. The only person she met was a solemn maid, who silently showed her to the prince's bedroom door and left her there.

The prince was lying in a large, comfortable bed. He was younger than the princess had imagined – about her own age – with a kind face. He was also fast asleep.

The princess sat down at his bedside to wait. Outside, she could hear voices calling in the little fishing village just beyond the castle walls, and the shrieking of seagulls over the cliffs. Inside, in the dim light that crept through the curtains, she listened to the ticking of the clock and the prince's soft breathing.

The princess realized with a sigh that she was stuck inside a castle once again. So she did what she always did. She began to tell a story to pass the time.

The long hours of waiting blurred into each other as her story took shape. She imagined that she and the prince were setting off on a grand adventure. She was surprised by just how quickly time passed.

That evening, and every evening, the maid brought

her food to eat and water to drink.

Each morning, she took up her story again, and the next day, and the next. Days passed and the prince snoozed on. Meanwhile, the princess's story blossomed. Together, they climbed volcanoes and dived deep into sunken cities. Together, they crossed storm-tossed seas and trackless, dusty deserts. Together, they found fabulous treasure, ferocious monsters and forbidden secrets.

Weeks and months slipped by. Seasons came and went. The princess never left the prince's bedside. She always watched his face – hoping for some small sign that he heard her story – but he never stirred, or twitched a lip. He didn't even snore.

But slowly, slowly, a strange thing was happening. Little by little, the princess began to feel that she knew what the prince was going to say and want to do. She knew that he was brave, but maybe a little rash. She knew that he liked dogs, swimming by moonlight, and cheese and pickle sandwiches. Slowly, slowly, little by little, the princess grew to love the silent prince.

Finally, one day, she heard sweet music and the crackle of fireworks outside. The village and the castle were celebrating the Midsummer festival at last. But the princess had been telling her story for so long, she had no idea that the day she had so long awaited had finally arrived.

"Why don't you go out onto the balcony and

listen?" suggested the maid, who'd just come in with the evening meal.

The princess was worried that the prince might wake up and not find her by his side, but she loved music very much. So she leaned over the balcony to hear the first music she had heard in many months.

"How beautiful it is," she murmured.

At that moment, the prince opened his eyes. The first person he saw was the maid. Of course, he assumed she must be the storyteller who had so enchanted his dreams.

"Are you the princess who has woken me from the enchantment?" he asked.

"Yes, I am!" said the maid, seizing her chance – and who could blame her?

"No!" cried the princess, rushing back in. "I am the princess!"

The prince had been asleep for a year, and was still feeling a little groggy.

"Here's a pretty puzzle," he muttered, looking from one girl to the other. "You can't both be the princess." Then he smiled. "I know! Answer me this: what was the name of the old hermit crab with stinky breath who lived at the bottom of the sea?"

"I don't know," said the maid. "What a very strange question."

"His name was Canute," said the princess with a huge grin.

"I loved that part of your story," said the prince. "He was an extremely silly crab."

"You heard it all?" asked the princess, walking over to the bed.

"I dreamed every word." The prince took her hand and looked into her eyes. "Thank you for breaking the curse – but thank you even more for your story."

They were both far too happy to be angry with the maid.

"Do you remember the time we singed the warlock's beard with a red-hot toasting fork?" asked the prince. "I thought that was a really clever idea."

The princess and the prince discussed the story long into the night and over the following days. Soon, they sent out invitations to their wedding.

The princess's parents, who had been worried sick, were delighted to hear that she was safe.

"She's even found herself a suitable husband too!" roared the king, after he opened her letter at breakfast. "I told you we needn't have worried."

"You said no such thing," replied the queen.

The whole kingdom was invited to their wedding, along with the Sun and the Stars and the Wind (and their mothers). The castle, which had been silent for so long, was filled with music and happy laughter and the rich smell of feasting.

Once they were married, the princess and the prince continued to tell their story. Each evening, after a hard day's ruling side by side, they sat together on a high balcony, looking out over the cliffs and waves. While they ate their supper, they took turns telling the story, weaving tales around tales, creating a pattern as fine and intricate as the stars that shone in the sky.

Once children arrived, these tales became their bedtime stories. As soon as they were old enough to join in, they added their own threads to the weave, which grew richer every day in the telling.

And even after the princess and the prince had been married for many years, they were still very much in love, for he had imagined her while dreaming, and she had dreamed of him while she was awake.

This fairy tale is based on 'The Ungrateful Dwarf'
by Caroline Stahl and its retelling
by the Brothers Grimm.

Snow White and Rose Red

Once there were two sisters, Snow White and Rose Red. They were named for the rose trees that grew in their garden – one as fair as Snow White's skin, the other with soft red petals that matched the bloom in Rose Red's cheeks.

The sisters were as different as night and day. Snow White loved to stay inside and read by the fire. She could weave baskets from rushes and carve creatures from wood.

Rose Red was happiest roaming the forest outside their home. She was as nimble as a deer and as swift as a bird. In summer, she collected wild berries and herbs, and dreamed of adventure in far-flung lands.

But even though the sisters were so different, they loved each other very much.

Every night, their mother would say, "Lock the door, children." And then they would curl up by the fire and their mother would open a book and begin, "Once upon a time..."

She told them stories of brave princesses and fire-breathing dragons, of glass mountains and marble palaces, with turrets that touched the sky.

"One day I'll go on an adventure," Rose Red would say.

"And I'll stay here at home with you, Mother,"

Snow White would add.

Then one night, in deepest winter, when the snow lay thick upon the ground, there came a KNOCK! KNOCK! KNOCK! at the door.

"Quick! Open the door, children," said their mother. "There must be a stranger out in the snow. They'll be half-frozen to death, for the wind is howling down from the mountains and the air is bitterly cold."

Rose Red hurried to the door, but when she opened it, she cried out. For there, more than twice her size, tall, sharp-clawed, with huge dark eyes, was a bear.

"Do not be afraid," said the bear, in a low, growling voice. "I will not hurt you.

I have come only to seek shelter from the cold," he explained.

Rose Red froze for a moment in surprise. Snow White darted behind a chair. But their mother came forward with outstretched hands. "Come in! Come in!" she said. "Warm yourself by our fire."

The bear dropped to all fours and padded inside. CRASH! went the table and down fell the chairs. His body seemed enormous in the little cottage, his breath as loud as the wind.

The two girls looked at each other and gasped. "You're letting him in, Mother?" they asked.

"All strangers are welcome here," their mother replied. "Besides, I do not think he is as fearsome as he seems."

At first, the girls were doubtful. But the bear's expression was so gentle and his eyes were so sad, that Snow White and Rose Red soon lost any fear.

Rose Red fetched a broom and brushed the snow from his fur. Snow White covered him with a warm blanket.

"Thank you," said the
bear. Then he lay down by
the fire and closed his eyes.

The mother went on with her story. Soon, the
cottage was filled with the bear's deep, rumbling
snores. He slept all night by the fire.

In the morning, Snow White unbolted the door
and with a growly, "Thank you," the bear padded
outside, his great dark body stark against the snow.

"Do you think he'll come back?" the girls asked
their mother.

"How can he talk?"

"Is he enchanted?"

"Or under a wicked spell?"

"Hush now," said their mother, smiling. "If the bear does return, you must take care not to ask him any questions. He will tell us what he wants us to know."

All day, the sisters hoped for the bear's return, and as night fell, they were rewarded.

Just as they were settling down to read by the fire, there came again a KNOCK! KNOCK! KNOCK! at the door. When Rose Red rushed to open it, there was the bear, standing on his hind legs, his great, heavy head peering into the cottage.

After that, he came every night, all through the snowy winter and into the spring.

Rose Red and Snow White loved to ride on his back.

They tickled the soft fur on his stomach and stroked his great head when he slept by the fire.

But as spring turned to summer, the bear sighed and said, "This is the last time you'll see me. I will not return tonight. I must go to the forest and stay there until winter comes."

"But why?" said Rose Red.

"Oh please don't leave us," begged Snow White.

"I have no choice," the bear replied. "Long ago, a wicked creature stole everything that was precious to me, and then put me under a curse. In winter, the creature hides underground, but in summer he returns to the forest. Every year I try to find him, to see if I can take back what is mine and break the curse. I cannot tell you any more, or the curse will last forever."

Snow White and Rose Red rushed over to hug the bear, and stroke his great head one last time.

"Thank you for looking after me," said the bear, "and for keeping me warm through the winter. Your kindness has warmed my heart."

With those words, the bear bounded through the little door of their cottage. As he went, his fur caught on the door and tore. Snow White was sure she saw a sudden flash of gold, bright and shining. The next moment, he was gone.

That night, the cottage seemed empty without him. And as one week passed, and then another, Snow White, Rose Red and their mother all spoke of how much they missed the bear – his rumbling voice, his warmth, his sad black eyes – though Snow White missed him most of all.

"I wish we could help him," she said to Rose Red one day.

"Perhaps we can," Rose Red replied. "Let's go into the forest and see if we can find him."

"May we, Mother?" asked Snow White.

Their mother looked up from her sewing with a sigh. "You must do what is right," she said. "But stay together and keep safe. Light a fire at night to keep away the wolves. If you are not back in three days, I shall come looking for you."

At once, the girls packed their bags. They took cloaks to cover themselves at night, a rod to catch fish and a tinderbox to light a fire.

"A real adventure at last!" said Rose Red.

They hugged their mother goodbye and set out into the forest.

They walked all day along winding paths. Just as the sun was starting to set, they rounded a corner to the sharp cry of, "Help me! Help me!"

The sisters ran forwards and there was a little goblin, his beard tangled in brambles. He was jumping up and down, squawking and shrieking, his face red with exertion and rage.

"Well don't just stand there!" shouted the goblin. "Do something!"

Rose Red reached into her pocket and pulled out a pair of scissors. SNIP! SNIP! SNIP! she went, the silvery blades flashing in the sun.

Tufts of the goblin's beard floated away on the wind like thistledown, until at last he was free.

"You fool!" cried the goblin. "You imbecile! That was the best part of my beard. I didn't ask you to cut it, did I?"

As he spoke, he bent down and snatched up a
sack by his feet. Rose Red thought she saw a flash
of gold, but then the goblin swung the sack over
his shoulder and strode away, muttering, "My poor,
poor beard... those silly, foolish girls..."

"Well!" huffed Rose Red, with her hands on her
hips, watching him go. "Of all the ungrateful..."

"I know," added Snow White. "He didn't even
say thank you."

"He didn't deserve our help," said Rose Red.
"We should have left him there, jumping up and
down, like an angry grasshopper."

The girls laughed and walked on a little way,
but by now darkness was beginning to settle over
the forest. "Let's find somewhere safe to sleep,"
suggested Snow White. "I don't think I can walk
any further."

Rose Red led them to a sandy bank beneath the
branches of a great oak tree. "We can rest here for
the night," she said. "I'll make a fire to keep the
wolves away."

When the fire was lit, they sat down and covered themselves with their cloaks. Snow White handed out the bread and cheese they had brought from home and told stories, while Rose Red gazed up at the shining stars and the round white moon. Then at last, Snow White fell silent and they curled up together and slept.

Dawn broke clear and bright above them. Rose Red stood and listened to the wind, then she pointed west. "I can hear the rushing of a river," she said. "Let's go and wash and then catch a fish for our breakfast."

They followed the sound until they came to the banks of a wide river. But there was the little goblin, pulling and tugging, muttering and mumbling, his beard caught in the twine of his fishing line.

"Oh jiminy-fidgety-higgedy-crickets," he muttered to himself. Then he looked up.

"Not you two again," he stormed. "Well, you'll have to do. Untangle me. Come on! What are you waiting for? Aren't you going to help?"

Rose Red darted forward with her scissors and with a SNIP! SNIP! SNIP! the goblin was free once more.

"You fiend!" cried the goblin, shaking his fists at them. "You've cut more of my beard. My beautiful beard." Then he reached down to grab the sack at his feet, before swinging it over his shoulder. "Fools," he said, as he hurried away. "Don't you dare come near my beard again or you'll be sorry!"

"Ruder and ruder," said Snow White, watching him go. "We should have left him by the river, leaping about like a salmon."

Laughing together, the girls went down to the river to wash. Rose Red caught a fish for their breakfast, which they cooked over a little fire. They spent the day wandering the forest paths.

That night, Rose Red lit another fire and the sisters lay down to sleep on a bed of ferns.

"We've been gone for two days now," said Rose Red, wrapping herself in her cloak.

"And we're running out of food," said Snow White. "Do you think we'll ever find the bear?"

"Do you want to go back?" asked Rose Red.

But Snow White shook her head. "We must find him," she said. "He's in trouble – I feel it."

The next morning, they woke with the sun and feasted on nuts and berries. Rose Red found wood sorrel for them to eat, growing in clumps on the forest floor. Then they gathered their things and walked deeper into the forest.

The oaks and birches gave way to spiky pine trees, their trunks growing tall and straight and tightly packed together. The air was cooler here, and darker, and the soft needles on the ground seemed to shift beneath their feet.

There was a little stream, and beyond it, a clearing. High ahead, they could see an eagle, circling and calling on outstretched wings. Suddenly, the eagle plunged down and there came a sharp cry.

Snow White and Rose Red ran towards the sound... and gasped. The eagle had caught the goblin by the shoulders and was gripping him with its talons. It flapped its wings again and again, desperately trying to carry the goblin away.

"HELP ME!" screeched the goblin, real terror in his voice. "Why aren't you helping, you dithering fools!"

The eagle flapped its wings again, this time lifting up the goblin, higher and higher, until his feet were dangling just above their heads.

...for a moment all three were lifted off the ground.

"What are you waiting for?" cried the goblin.

At once, Rose Red leaped up and grabbed the goblin by the foot, but still the eagle wouldn't let go. Snow White took hold of the other foot and for a moment all three were lifted off the ground.

The sisters tugged and heaved until at last, with a final screech, the eagle released its grip and they all came tumbling to earth.

The goblin got to his feet first, huffing and puffing and brushing himself down.

"What were you doing, tugging on me like that?" he complained. "You're so clumsy, both of you." He scowled at them, then looked around for his sack, which was lying close by. He checked it carefully and Rose Red saw it was now full to the brim with gold and jewels.

"I hope I never have the misfortune to meet you again," said the ungrateful goblin, turning to go. But before Rose Red could answer back, a growl rang through the trees. Both Rose Red and Snow White turned, but neither felt afraid.

"Stop him!" called a familiar voice. "Don't let him get away!"

Over the ridge came the bear, just visible between the trees.

For a moment, the goblin froze, then he grabbed his sack and started to run. The sisters chased him, but the goblin was too quick, darting this way and that, his breath coming in quick pants.

Behind them, they could hear the bear, his heavy feet pounding the forest floor. At last, Rose Red lunged forward and caught the goblin by his silvery beard.

The goblin let out a cry, pulling and tugging, kicking and fighting, but Rose Red refused to let go.

"Release me, you fool!" cried the goblin. "Or I'll make you regret it. No one crosses a goblin and gets away with it."

But Rose Red clung on, and moments later, the bear reached them. He rose up onto his hind legs, towering above them, his great paws raised.

"Give me back my treasure," he growled at the goblin, "and I'll let you go free."

With trembling hands, the goblin flung his sack to the ground. "I always feared you'd catch up with me one day," he said. Then he spun around and fled into the forest.

The bear dropped to all fours. He thrust his paw into the sack and pulled out a golden cloak. "At last," he said, and turned to the girls.

"Close your eyes," he commanded, "and look away until I say."

Snow White and Rose Red did as he asked, covering their eyes with their hands. There followed a blinding flash of light.

"It's safe to look now," came the voice again, only it was less growly than before.

The girls opened their eyes to find the bear had

vanished. In his place stood a prince, dressed in gleaming gold, his cloak billowing behind him.

"What happened?" asked Snow White. "Was it the goblin? Was he the evil creature who put you under a curse?"

The prince nodded. "Many years ago, the goblin stole my treasure. Then he turned me into a bear and trapped me in the forest. The only way to break the curse was to find the goblin and take back my golden cloak."

"For many years I lived alone," the prince went on. "Until that coldest of winters, when your family took me in. And now you have helped me catch the goblin. Without you, I never would have won back my human form."

The prince and the sisters walked through the forest to their cottage. The sisters kept glancing at the prince, as if they couldn't believe that this was their bear, transformed.

When at last they reached home, their mother came rushing out to greet them.

She threw her arms around her daughters. "I'm
so glad to have you back," she said. "A moment
longer and I should have come looking for you."

She turned to the prince, looking deep into his
large, dark eyes.

"Do you recognize me?" he asked.

"I do," said the mother, smiling. And the prince
told her his story.

"In return for your kindness," he said, "I'd like
you all to come and stay in my palace for a while."

"Oh! May we?" asked Snow White, looking to
her mother.

"Of course," her mother replied.

The prince left that day, promising to send for
them as soon as he reached his home. And the next
morning, true to his word, a royal carriage arrived,
with four white horses, tossing their heads, and a
coachman to drive them.

The years passed. Snow White and Rose Red
went often to visit the prince at his palace. In time,
Snow White and the prince fell deeply in love and

decided to marry. Princes came to the wedding from all over the kingdom and many asked for Rose Red's hand in marriage. But to each one, she said no.

After the wedding, she turned to her mother and sister. "It is time for me to go. Your home is here at the palace but I still long to explore."

"Are you sure you won't stay?" asked Snow White, tears in her eyes.

Rose Red shook her head and hugged them both goodbye.

Then she walked out of the palace and into her life of adventure. For all we know, she is exploring still...

This fairy tale is based on an old Scottish tale collected by Joseph Jacobs and Flora Annie Steele, who give Molly's full name as Molly Whuppie.

Clever Molly

It had been a long, hard winter, and food was scarce. Molly's house was full of empty cupboards and emptier stomachs. At dinner time, she and her sisters stared at empty plates. Then, late that night, she overheard her parents talking in worried tones...

"We've almost nothing left to eat," said her mother, heaving a deep sigh.

"If only we had fewer mouths to feed," replied her father sadly. "With you and me *and* the girls, I simply don't know how we're going to survive until spring..."

Molly had a ready answer. She put her head around the door and said, "Why then, let me go and seek my fortune!"

Her mother and father shook their heads. "We would rather starve than send you away."

"Starving won't help anyone," Molly pointed out. "Please!"

All the talking woke Molly's two sisters, who demanded to know what was going on.

"Molly wants to go and seek her fortune," said their mother.

"Because we haven't enough food left to feed us all," explained their father.

"And because it'll be an adventure!" added Molly, with a laugh.

At the idea of an adventure, the sisters decided they wanted to go too – and they and Molly were so determined that, in the end, their parents reluctantly had to agree.

Early next morning, the three sisters set off, following the old country road that wound past their house.

"Wherever it leads," said Molly, "we can't be hungrier than here."

They walked up hill and down dale, and away from all the places they knew. They walked and walked until their legs ached – and then they walked some more. As they went on, the land around them grew wilder. After a long while, they reached a forest. Huge, dark trees rose all around, but the path continued between the trees, so they kept walking.

It was a long time since they had seen any signs of other people. At last, as the day began to fade, they glimpsed a welcoming light.

"Look!" cried Molly, pointing.

Clever Molly

Deep among the trees stood a high stone building, its windows glowing in the dusk.

"It's a house," said Molly. "We can ask for food there."

As the girls drew closer, they realized the house was enormous – easily twice as high as a normal house.

Molly's sisters hung back. "It looks like a giant's house," they said nervously.

Clever Molly

"So I will ask for some GIANT food," laughed Molly, marching straight up to the huge front door.

Rat-a-tat-tat! She rapped firmly on the rough wooden planks.

The door creaked open and a woman peered out. To the sisters' relief, she was an ordinary-sized woman, with a kindly expression – but she shook her head and frowned when she saw Molly on the doorstep.

"What on earth are you doing here?" she exclaimed. "Don't you know my husband is a giant? If he sees three little girls like you, he'll eat you up as soon as look at you!"

"Please, ma'am, my sisters and I are STARVING," pleaded Molly. "Can you spare anything to eat?"

The woman hesitated. She hated to see anyone go hungry, and the sisters reminded her of her own three daughters... After a moment she nodded. "All right, come in. But hurry! You will have to be gone before my husband comes home."

Inside, by the fire, three girls – the giant's daughters – were eating bowls of bread and milk. The woman crumbled fresh bread into three more bowls and added creamy milk from a large earthenware jug.

Molly and her sisters settled down to munch contentedly – but they had barely lifted their spoons when the floor shook with giant footsteps.

Thump…

thump…

thump…

BANG!

The door crashed open, revealing a towering figure, almost twice as high as Molly's own father, with fierce eyes and crooked teeth. The giant had come home early.

He stepped inside and sniffed the air.

Fee, fi, fo, fum,

I smell the blood of a human… YUM!

His wife shook her head firmly. "Now dear,

there's no blood," she said. "Just these three little girls here, Molly and her sisters, that I invited in to eat with us."

"Thank you for the food," said Molly, getting up quickly. "Now we must be going…"

"Oh no," interrupted the giant, slamming the door quickly. "It's much too late to be going anywhere; you must spend the night with us. You can sleep beside my daughters."

He gave Molly and her sisters a lopsided grin. But moments later, Molly saw him lick his lips hungrily and remembered the woman's warning.

"We have to get out of here," she thought. "But not while the giant is watching." So she sat and ate with her sisters, and smiled and chatted with the giant's daughters as if they were all old friends.

At bedtime, the giant announced he had a present for each of his daughters. He reached into his pocket and pulled out three pretty necklaces of sparkling gold chain, which he placed proudly around their necks.

"But we mustn't forget our guests," he added. "Hmm... let me see." He took three wisps of straw, and twisted them and braided them, until he had made three more necklaces. "So you don't feel left out," he said gruffly, giving one each to Molly and her sisters.

Molly watched the giant carefully. She didn't trust him one little bit. "He's up to something with these necklaces," she thought to herself. But out loud, all she said was: "Thank you."

When they finally went to bed, Molly waited until the other girls were sound asleep. Very quietly, so as not to wake anyone, she swapped the necklaces so she and her sisters had the gold chains, and the giant's daughters had the straw. Then she lay down and pretended to snore.

In the dark of night, a giant shadow stole into the girls' room and a giant hand stretched out, feeling for the necklaces... When it touched straw, it seized that girl and stuffed her headfirst into a sack. The girls with gold chains the hand left sleeping peacefully.

"This'll make a tasty breakfast!" the giant gloated to himself, as he tied up the bulging sack, ignoring the outraged cries from within. He hefted it onto his shoulders and crept away to lock it in his larder.

Molly lay wide-eyed in the dark, hardly daring to move, until she heard giant snores rumbling from the other room. Then she let out a deep breath and sat up. She nudged her sisters until they blinked awake.

"Time to go!" she hissed in an urgent undertone.

The three sisters tiptoed out of the giant's house and ran and ran through the moonlit forest, until they came to a deep ravine. Far below, a river roared and tumbled over jagged rocks. Ahead of them stretched a rope so fine, it was like a hair.

"There's no bridge," exclaimed one sister.

"What shall we do?" said the other.

"Why, use the rope," said Molly. "Look!"

She ran lightly across, to show them. "It's just like walking across a bridge, really," she said to encourage the others, as they inched their way carefully along it. "I shall call it the Bridge of One Hair."

When the sisters reached the far side, they kept

❧ Clever Molly ❧

"I shall call it the Bridge of One Hair."

walking until, at dawn, they came to a castle. Strong stone walls towered above them and bright flags rippled in the breeze.

A guard stood by the gate. "Where did you three spring from?" he asked.

"Through the forest and over the Bridge of One Hair," said Molly.

The guard stared. "But didn't you meet the wicked giant?"

"Oh yes," said Molly cheerfully.

The guard shook his head in amazement. "You'd better come with me," he said. "I know the king will want to see you."

He led Molly and her sisters down a long, carpeted corridor and into a lofty throne room. With a low bow, he introduced the sisters and explained how they had arrived.

"How did you get through the forest?" asked the king at once. "Didn't you meet the wicked giant along your way?"

"Oh yes," said Molly. "He tried to eat us,

but we escaped."

The king's eyes widened. "You escaped from the giant! Not many can make that claim – and you're just a child! You must have great brains and even greater bravery."

The king sighed. "Even my best soldiers fear the giant. Only the rope bridge keeps him from ransacking the lands on this side of the river, for he cannot cross the ravine. Oh how I wish we could defeat him for good..."

"Perhaps I could help?" said Molly.

The king gave her a serious look. "It would be very dangerous," he warned.

Molly shrugged. "I don't mind a bit of danger," she said cheerfully.

The king nodded. "Very well," he said. "Listen... the giant relies on three magical treasures to give him his strength: a sword of iron, a purse of silver and a ring of gold. You will need to steal all three. If you succeed in ridding my people of this constant threat, I'll – why, I'll give you half my kingdom!"

"Very well," said Molly. "I'll try." Her tummy rumbled. "But I'll need a good breakfast first!"

The king nodded and snapped his fingers. "Summon the cook!" he commanded.

That day, the sisters feasted on stacks of buttery toast, scrambled eggs and sweet pancakes, washed down with flagons of orange juice. They thought they had never tasted anything so delicious.

At nightfall, Molly crept back to the giant's house. Through the window, she could see a huge iron sword hanging on the wall above the fire. She waited until the giant was snoring.

Then she tiptoed inside and reached up...

Clitter-clatter!

The blade shook inside the scabbard, and the giant sprang awake.

Quick as thought, Molly grabbed the sword and ran. She ran back to the rope bridge and across it, and the giant could not follow.

"Woe to you, Molly," he yelled, shaking a giant fist at her. "Never come this way again!"

Molly shrugged, quite unafraid. "I'll be back twice more," she replied boldly.

The next night, Molly returned for the purse – a large leather pouch, stuffed full of heavy silver coins. She saw the giant tuck it under his pillow before he went to sleep. Once he was snoring, she tiptoed in and reached out...

Chink-clink!

The coins in the pouch shifted, and the giant sprang awake. He snatched at her – too late. Molly was already running.

Quick as thought, she ran back to the rope bridge and across it, leaving the giant waving his fist after her. "Woe to you, Molly," he yelled angrily. "Never come this way again!"

"I'll be back once more," she called out, as bold as brass.

On the third night, Molly came for the ring. This was a band of gold the size of a small bracelet, and Molly knew exactly where she would find it, because the giant always wore it on his thumb.

This time, the giant snored louder than ever when he went to bed... or perhaps he was only pretending. For as soon as Molly tiptoed in and tugged off the ring, he sprang up and seized her. Molly wiggled and squirmed, but she couldn't break free – the giant's grip was like iron.

"Aha, I've caught you, you pesky thief!" crowed the giant. "I guess you're not so clever after all. Now, what shall I do with you?"

Molly thought fast. "If I were you," she said quickly, "I'd tie me in a sack, so I couldn't escape. And then I'd go out and find a stick, to beat me black and blue."

"Very well," said the giant, with a nasty chuckle. "I will!"

He stuffed Molly headfirst into a sack, ring and all. Then he tied the top tightly and went to look for a stick, slamming the door firmly shut behind him...

BANG!

As soon as the giant had left, Molly began to sing loudly and merrily inside the sack.

Oh, if you could see what I can see...

"What CAN you see?" asked the giant's wife, coming in to see what all the noise was about.

Molly didn't reply. She just kept on singing, as loud and merry as before.

Oh, if you could see what I can see...

The giant's wife itched with curiosity.

"I must see this for myself," she thought. "It must be something utterly amazing, to make Molly sing out like that."

So she took a pair of scissors and cut open the sack, in order to take Molly's place inside it herself...

Molly was free!

Quick as thought, she was up and running – taking the giant's gold ring with her.

Thump...

thump...

thump...

The giant came stomping back, carrying a stout new stick. He was just about to give the sack a mighty thwack when his wife popped her head out, shook the dust from her hair and complained: "I see nothing but sackcloth!"

"What are YOU doing in there?" roared the giant, dropping the stick in surprise. "Where's that thief, Molly?"

Just then, he glimpsed Molly out of the window and, with an angry roar, ran after her.

He ran and ran, and Molly ran and ran, until they came to the Bridge of One Hair. Molly ran over, just as easily as before, but the giant had to stop.

"Woe to you, Molly," yelled the giant furiously. "NEVER come this way again!"

"Nor shall I," said Molly, grinning merrily. "Not now I have this." And she held up the ring in triumph.

The gold glittered in the rays of the sun, which was just coming over the horizon, and the giant saw he was defeated. He roared again – but this time, all that came out was a squeak. His power was finally broken.

As for Molly, she went back to the king and presented him proudly with the ring.

"I don't think the giant will give you any more trouble," she said.

The king beamed at her. "Then you have earned your reward," he said. "Just as I promised, half my kingdom is yours!"

Now Molly was rich enough to build a castle of her own, where she and her sisters lived happily with their parents until the end of their days... and none of them ever went hungry again.

This fairy tale is Scottish. It was collected by Andrew and Nora Lang in the Orkney Islands and first published in 1889.

Kate Crackernuts

Once upon a time there was a king with a beautiful daughter, named Anna. The king's wife had died soon after Anna's birth, but he and his daughter lived happily together in a castle on the edge of a moor. In summer, they watched the heather burst into flower. In winter, they sat by the fire as the snow turned the world to white.

One misty morning, a woman arrived at the castle with a small daughter of her own.

"My name is Eleanor," said the woman, her daughter hiding behind her skirts.

"And this is my daughter, Kate." Her voice was as soft as the morning breeze. Her hair was raven black and her eyes were as green as the birch leaves. But there was something about the woman that Anna did not like. No sooner had the king seen her, however, than he fell deeply in love.

"You and your daughter are welcome to stay at my castle," he said, as if bewitched. "Stay as long as you wish."

"It's as if Father's under a spell," thought Anna. And she noticed that the mist that had swept in with Eleanor clung to the castle like a cloak. It stayed for days, then weeks, muffling their footsteps on the cold stone floors, masking the world beyond.

In that time, the king rarely left Eleanor's side. He hung on her words, his eyes never leaving her face, as if everything else had ceased to exist for him. And then, one morning, Anna woke to the news that her father had asked Eleanor to be his wife, and to his delight, she had accepted.

As soon as the wedding was over, the new queen turned wicked and vain. She demanded the king hand over his money, then spent it all on rich furnishings for her rooms, until there was barely enough left to buy food. She was beastly to her daughter and most horrible of all to Anna.

"Take care," she would say, scowling at her, "that you never grow more beautiful than me... For that way danger lies."

Anna noticed how the queen only seemed truly happy in front of her mirror, losing herself in the beauty of her own reflection. As for her father – he was never the same again. The mist outside the castle was like a mist over his mind. He could see no wrong in his queen.

Though Anna hated her stepmother, she adored Kate like a sister. As children, they romped down the long corridors and played hide-and-seek among the twisting turrets. Together they dreamed of life outside the castle walls. "One day we'll escape," they promised each other. "Together, we'll explore the world beyond the misty moor."

On Anna's eighteenth birthday, the king died, and the wicked queen began to plot and plan. "Anna has grown too beautiful," she whispered to her maid one day. "Something must be done."

"Why don't you visit the henwife in the village," said the maid. "She can heal with herbs and enchant with potions made from flowers. Some say she even knows magic…"

That night, the queen left the castle under cover of darkness, wrapped in an old cloak. When she returned, she was smiling.

"Anna, dear," she said, the next morning, "I would like you to go to the village across the moor and visit the henwife. Give her this basket of food and then make sure you hurry back," she crooned.

Anna was suspicious, but she was too frightened of the queen to disobey. She set out across the moor, the mist hanging close around her, until at last the village came into view. She knocked on the henwife's door.

"Come in, come in," said the henwife. "I've been expecting you." She took the basket of food and led Anna to a pot, bubbling over the stove. "You must be hungry, after that long walk. Please, my dear, have a taste of my soup."

The henwife lifted the lid from the pot. Anna bent down and there was a sudden clap of thunder and a flash of light. In an instant, Anna no longer had her pretty face...

In an instant, Anna no longer had her pretty face...
Instead, she had the head of a sheep!

Instead, she had the head of a sheep!

"Whaaat have you done?" wailed Anna, catching sight of her reflection in the cooking pot.

"What I have done cannot be undone by me," chuckled the henwife.

Anna clutched at her fuzzy head, tears streaming down her cheeks. Then she fled back to the castle.

"Kaaate! Kaaaaate!" she bleated, as soon as she got home. "You have to help me."

As soon as Kate saw her sister, she knew what had happened. "This must be my mother's work. Don't worry. I'll find a way to change you back."

Then she took a scarf from her drawer and wrapped it around Anna's head. Next, she gave her a long, hooded cloak. "This will keep you warm and hide your face," she said. "We'll leave straight away. I'll find you a cure, I promise."

Kate and Anna left the castle, walking for many days and many nights, down dusty roads and through dark forests.

"I'm so tired," said Anna, dragging her feet. "Perhaps it is part of the henwife's spell, but all I want to do is sleep."

"Don't worry," said Kate. "I'll find a safe place for us to rest. Look! There's a castle just beyond these woods. Let's see if they'll let us stay." And she took Anna's hand and led her through the trees.

Kate knocked on the great wooden door, while Anna hid her face beneath her hooded cloak.

A servant answered. "Good day," he said, sneeringly, taking in Kate's muddy shoes, her wind-blown hair. He barely cast a glance at Anna. "What can I do for you?"

"Could you tell me who lives here?" asked Kate.

"The old king and his son," replied the servant. "But the king doesn't open his doors to visitors. The prince is sick and the king does not like him to be disturbed."

"Please take us to the king," said Kate. "Tell him I may be able to help his son."

"Wait here while I see," the servant replied.

The king agreed to meet them, and the girls curtseyed before him. "Your Majesty," said Kate. "May we stay the night? My sister is sick and in need of rest."

"My son is also sick," replied the king. "He sleeps all day and never stirs. All who watch over him vanish before morning comes. If I let you rest with your sister, will you guard my son? Will you take that risk?"

"I will," promised Kate. "In return, I ask for ten pieces of silver."

The king looked at Kate for a long while, but she held up her chin and met his gaze.

"I am stronger than I look," she said. "You need not fear for your son while he is under my watch.

The king nodded in reply. "Then I agree."

The king called for a maid, who showed
Anna to a fine room with a crackling fire. As
soon as the servants had left, Kate led Anna to
the four-poster bed.

"Rest now, sister," she said, pulling the covers
over her. "I will find a cure."

That night, Kate sat by the sleeping prince. He
lay there, pale and still, and for many hours he did
not stir. Then, as the clock struck midnight, he rose
from his bed and slipped downstairs. Kate followed
as quietly as she could. She need not have worried.
It was as if the prince was walking in his sleep,
with no sense that she was there.

"There is magic at work here," thought Kate.
"But who has cast this spell?"

Outside, the moon shone bright. The prince
strode to the stables and saddled his horse, then
galloped into the night. Quickly, Kate saddled a
horse of her own and rode after him.

Kate followed the prince across green fields,
along rushing rivers and through wooded glades.

As they trotted beneath the trees, Kate reached out
and plucked nuts from the branches, slipping them
into her pocket.

At last, the prince came to a halt by a green hill.
He swung down from his horse and whispered,

> *Land of fairies, land of sprites,*
> *Open up this moonlit night.*

Even as the words left his lips, a gap opened
in the hill. The prince tethered his horse to a tree
and slid through the gap, with Kate following close
behind him.

Inside, was a magnificent hall, lit with flaming torches. A hundred fairies danced to violins. They smiled when they saw the prince and held out their hands to him. "Come and join us," they sang, though they looked at Kate without seeing her.

The prince ran to the fairies and joined their dance, his feet flying over the ground, his body swaying in time to the music.

The prince danced until he could dance no more. Then he dragged himself to a chair, where the fairies fanned him with their wings and plied him with nectar juice, until he rose to his feet and cried, "I am ready to dance again."

Kate watched from the shadows. She saw tables lined with delectable fairy food – honey cakes and rose syrup, golden nuts and silver berries – but she knew better than to eat them. Those who tasted fairy food never made it back to the outside world. Instead, she cracked the nuts in her pocket and feasted on them until dawn broke.

As the first light of day streamed into the hill, the fairies ceased their dancing. With a wave, and a promise to come again, the prince leaped onto his horse. He galloped home through wooded glades, along rushing rivers and across green fields, with Kate riding fast behind him.

By the time the old king entered his son's room, the prince was lying in bed, fast asleep. Kate sat beside him, cracking the nuts from her pocket.

"Kate, you're still here!" exclaimed the old king. "And how is my son?"

"The same as before," Kate replied, saying nothing of their midnight ride and the dancing fairies in the green hill.

"Will you watch over him again?" asked the delighted king.

"I will," said Kate. "But in return, I ask that you give me ten gold pieces."

The king agreed. Once he had left, Kate rushed to her sister's room and found her in bed, lying weak and still.

"I'm not sure I can get up," said Anna, taking her sister's hand. "Please, find me a cure soon..."

The second night passed just as the first. The prince slept until midnight, then saddled his horse. Again, Kate rode behind him, gathering nuts from the trees. Again, the prince galloped to the green hill and called out,

> *Land of fairies, land of sprites,*
> *Open up this moonlit night.*

Kate entered the hill behind the prince, but this time, she decided to explore. She found a snug little room, where fairy babies played, watched over by older fairies. One nodded towards a fairy baby who was clutching a glowing wand.

"Three strokes of that wand would make Kate's sister as pretty as ever," she said.

"Can it be true?" wondered Kate. She crouched down, took a nut from her pocket and rolled it towards the fairy baby. Just as she'd hoped, the baby dropped her wand and fluttered after the nut. Kate saw her chance and snatched up the wand.  Then she waited for dawn to break. At first light, she rode back to the castle beside the silent prince.

The next morning, the old king entered his son's bedroom to see Kate once again sitting beside the sleeping prince, cracking the nuts from her pocket.

"You have guarded him now for two nights," said the old king. "Will you watch my son again?"

"If I stay a third night, will you give me two of your finest horses?" asked Kate.

The king agreed.

"And what if I cure your son?" asked Kate.

"You think you can?" asked the king. "Do you know what has happened to him?"

"It's fairy magic," Kate replied. "I can say no more than that. But I think I can cure him."

"I'd give you anything," swore the king.

"A home for my sister and me?"

"You can have any house in the kingdom if you bring back my son," said the king.

As soon as the king left, Kate ran to her sister's room and found her sleeping deeply, her sheep's head resting on the soft white pillows.

Kate held her breath and tapped Anna three times with the fairy wand. At once, there was a clap as loud as thunder and a flash of light. The sheep's head vanished and there was Anna... just as beautiful as ever. She opened her eyes and flung her arms around her sister.

"Oh Kate," she cried. "You did it! Thank you!"

"Can we stay one more night?" asked Kate. "For then, I think, we might be truly free."

"Of course," said Anna, hugging her tight.

That night, Kate once again sat by the prince's side. At midnight, they rode together to the green hill, the prince as unseeing as ever.

As they went, Kate plucked the nuts from the trees. As before, when they reached the green hill, the prince cried,

Land of fairies, land of sprites,
Open up this moonlit night.

While the prince danced the night away, Kate went to the room where the fairy babies played. This time, she saw a baby with a barley stalk in her hands.

"Three sips of barley soup would cure the prince," said one of the older fairies.

As soon as she heard those words, Kate rolled a nut to the fairy baby, then snatched up the barley.

The night passed as all the others had done, but once Kate saw the prince was safely back in his bed, she hurried to her sister, and told her what she had heard.

"Then we must make the soup," said Anna. "It is not yet dawn. If we go now to the castle kitchens, the servants will still be in bed."

They hurried to the kitchens, where Anna

boiled the barley grains until they were tender, and Kate stirred them into a soup. Then Kate carried the bowl upstairs and fed the sleeping prince.

"Oh," said the prince, opening his eyes at the first sip. "I wish I could have another."

So Kate gave him another sip, and the prince sat up in bed. "Oh for another spoonful," he begged, and Kate gave him a third. This time, the prince sprang out of bed.

"I'm well again," he cried. "I'm truly well."

He looked at Kate, as if seeing her for the very first time. "Was it you who cured me? What did you do?"

And Kate told him the story, of the moonlit rides and the green hill, of the fairies and the dancing and the words she had overheard.

"Thank you," said the prince, "for breaking the fairy curse. I remember it all now, but it's as if it happened in a dream..."

Just then, the old king came into the room. He was overjoyed to see his son, standing tall and strong, his eyes awake to the world.

"Kate," he said, "you've given me back my child! Please, take the finest horses in my stables. Choose any house in my kingdom."

"Thank you," said Kate. "I'll leave you two alone now." And she hurried through to her sister's room.

"It worked!" she said. "The prince is cured. Now we can have the adventures we dreamed of, and then come back to a home of our own."

Anna held up the fairy wand. "There is just one thing I'd like to do first."

Together, the two sisters rode away from the castle, through dark forests and down dusty roads, until at last they came to their moor. It was high summer, but the purple heather was hidden under a cloak of mist and no bees buzzed between the flowers. Kate and Anna rode up to the castle door, now rusted with neglect.

Kate lifted the great iron handle and knocked. At last, the queen's maid opened the door. "Take us to my mother, please," said Kate.

The maid gasped when she saw Anna. "Are you sure?" she asked. "The queen won't be happy about this."

"We're sure," said Anna.

The maid led them up to the queen's bedchamber, where she sat before her mirror.

"How can this be?" cried the queen when she saw them. "How did you break the spell?"

Anna simply smiled and flicked the fairy wand. There was a clap as loud as thunder and a flash of light. In an instant, the wicked queen had a sheep's head.

"No!" she cried, gazing at herself in the mirror, horrified.

Kate and Anna turned to go. "Come baaaaack!" wailed the queen. "You can't leave me like this."

She ran after them, down the stairs, but as soon as Kate and Anna were outside, they flung themselves onto their horses, laughing, and galloped away across the moor. Even as they rode, they saw the mist was rising.

"Her evil magic must be fading," said Anna. "Where shall we go now?"

"Wherever we like," said Kate. "This is where our adventure begins..."

This fairy tale is based on a story first written down by Karl Mullenhoff. The Brothers Grimm later added it to their collection and called it 'Maid Maleen'.

The Nettle Princess

A long time ago and quite far away, two kingdoms were at war. No one could remember *why* they were at war, just that they had been for years and that was how things were.

Every month, knights marched to a hill between the kingdoms and fought a great battle, with swords swirling and spears hurling and people crying out, "For the king!" or, "To the death!" or, "Ow my eye!" while the king of each kingdom watched from a distance, trying to remember what this war was all about.

Below the hill sat a small forest, which belonged to neither kingdom and had grown wild and beautiful. Squirrels scampered through glades and deer darted between shafts of sunlight that pierced the thick canopy of trees.

Only two people ever entered this forest, and only at dawn, when both kingdoms were fast asleep. One was a princess named Elisa and the other was a prince named Hans, and they were deeply in love.

They met in secret because they were not allowed to be in love. Elisa was from one kingdom and Hans was from the other, and their fathers, the kings, were bitter enemies. They both adored the forest and had met while exploring its winding paths. They knew that they were supposed to be enemies, and should probably fight, but instead they fell in love.

Since then, Elisa and Hans had met every morning in the forest, where they could escape the misery of palace life. Neither of them could

stand wearing royal clothes or attending royal ceremonies, or any of the other silly royal things expected of them.

"My father wants me to wear pretty gowns and marry a knight," Elisa told Hans, with a frown.

"Mine wants me to fight in the war and wear velvet tunics," Hans muttered, sadly. "He said I should act like a prince."

"Act like a prince!" Elisa scoffed. "Promise me we'll never marry or fight or do any of those silly royal things? This forest is *our* kingdom."

Elisa smiled at a patch of nettles, which seemed to whisper as the plants swayed in the wind.

"Hello little nettles," she said. "How are you, this morning?"

Hans laughed. "You are the only person I know who talks to weeds," he joked.

"They're not weeds," Elisa replied, with a twinkle in her eye. "They are my friends."

Every day, Elisa's heart sank as she returned to her palace. It was a dull, formal place, full of dull formal people seeking to please her father.

"Elisa, stand up straight!" the king snapped, one day. "This is Lord Winklebury, my finest, and richest, knight."

Lord Winklebury bowed so low that his helmet fell off. "Princess, I am charmed."

Elisa wasn't charmed at all, but she forced a smile, letting her thoughts drift back to the forest and Hans...

"Lord Winklebury will be your husband," the king added.

Elisa blinked. "Excuse me?"

Lord Winklebury dipped into another extremely low bow. "It will be my privilege to take your hand, my princess."

Elisa burst out laughing. "You'll take no such thing," she said.

The king's cheeks flushed pink. "My dear, Lord Winklebury is our finest, *and richest*, knight."

"I don't care how fine or rich he is," Elisa replied. "I'm not marrying him."

Lord Winklebury rose, dizzy from his deep bow. "Why ever not?" he asked.

"Because I don't want to," Elisa replied. "I don't even know you. I certainly don't love you. I love Hans."

The words came out before she could stop them, and a gasp spread around the room.

The king sat up on his throne. His eyes almost popped out of his head. "I beg your pardon? What did you just say?" he demanded.

Elisa's hands trembled, but she refused to lie. "I am in love with Hans," she repeated, with as much courage as she could muster.

The king glared at her in fury as he rose slowly from his throne. "You are *not* in love with Hans," he insisted.

"But Father... I am."

"You are not! You will marry Lord Winklebury."

"Father, I won't."

The king began to shake with rage. He couldn't afford to look weak in front of his knights. "You will," he repeated, "or I shall send you to the Tower."

Another gasp swept around the room. The Tower was a punishment reserved for the kingdom's worst enemies.

Just the thought of the Tower made Elisa's heart beat double-time. But she would not lie, and she would not betray her love.

"I'm sorry, Father," she said, softly. "Do what you must do."

The king frowned at her, and for a moment the anger in his face was replaced by something softer, more like sadness. Then he roared to his guards. "Take her to the Tower until she changes her mind!"

The guards didn't need to take Elisa; she went freely, although she was desperately sad. Rain began to fall as they marched to a hill near the palace. A stone tower stood at its top, a bleak spear stabbing the stormy sky.

It was as gloomy a prison as you could imagine, without a single window. The guards dragged some barrels of water and sacks of oats through the only entrance, and then shoved Elisa in too.

"This is your last chance," the king bellowed from his horse. "Do you love Hans?"

Elisa smiled sadly. It would be easy to tell her

father what he wanted to hear, but it would be a lie. "Father," she replied, "you taught me to be truthful and brave. This is the truth, and as brave as I can be. Half of my heart belongs to you. The other half belongs to Hans."

The king's eyes watered, but he wiped the tears away, pretending it was rain. "Seal it up," he ordered.

With stones and mortar, the guards began to seal the entrance to the Tower.

Elisa didn't move. From where she stood, she could see right across the kingdom to the forest. She wondered if Hans was there now, waiting for her...

The last stone blocked her view, and Elisa was left alone in the dark. The walls were so thick she heard nothing other than her own scared, shallow breaths.

Minutes grew into hours, hours into days, and days turned into weeks. Elisa's hair became dirty and tangled, and her skin turned pale from so long in the dark. But she wasn't entirely alone. After several months, she spotted a tiny nettle growing where a smidge of light shone through the wall.

"Little nettle," Elisa croaked. "How nice it is to have a friend in here."

She sat with the nettle as months turned into a year. When her fingernails grew too long, she filed them on the mortar between the stones. She ate the oats and drank the water until there was little left of either.

"Oh nettle," she gasped. "Surely someone will bring more?"

She waited and waited, but no one came.

"Little nettle," she wheezed. "I fear I shall die here soon."

As if in reply, the nettle swayed. Elisa sat up, staring at her green friend. There was light where the nettle grew – was there a breeze too?

She moved closer and felt the cold stone. The mortar was thinner there than in other places. Elisa scratched at it with her nails, and some crumbled away.

For the first time since she had been imprisoned, her heart fluttered with hope. "Can I... escape?"

From that moment, there wasn't another thought in Elisa's head. She scratched at the mortar until her fingernails were blunt, and then waited for them to grow back. Then she scratched and waited again.

After several weeks, a single, needle-thin beam of light pierced the wall. Elisa slid back, startled by the golden shaft after so long in the dark.

"I scratched right through the mortar," she told the nettle, which rustled in reply.

After another month of scratching, several more rays of sunlight shone into the gloomy prison. At last, a stone began to wobble.

"Just in time," Elisa gasped – for her food and water had now run out.

She pressed her back against the stone. Then, with the last scraps of her strength, she pushed... and pushed...

The stone scraped back and fell away. Elisa clambered through the hole and thumped to the ground outside.

She rose, squinting in the dazzling daylight.

"The princess has escaped!" cried a shrill voice.

One of the king's knights had been riding past the Tower. He spotted Elisa and leaped from his horse. "I'll save you from the king's anger," he cried. "You can marry me!"

"No thank you," Elisa said.

"Well," the knight huffed, "then I shall catch you. For as long as I've courage in my heart, I– "

Elisa didn't hear the rest; she was already running. Her legs were thin and weak, but her heart was still strong. She staggered down the hill to a hay barn, where another knight was combing his hair. He saw Elisa and dropped to one knee.

"Marry me!" he called.

Elisa kept running, across a meadow to a windmill, where a third knight sat polishing his chain mail.

"Marry me!" he begged. "Please?"

The knights chased Elisa to the forest. She splashed through puddles, leaped fallen branches, and hid, gasping, among a patch of nettles.

The knights scampered around the forest, searching for Elisa as they squabbled over which of them would marry her and become the king's son-in-law. None of them dared look among the nettles.

"Those nettles look quite sting-y," one of them muttered.

Eventually, disappointed, they trotted off. Elisa sighed so hard the nettles swayed and brushed her skin. But not one plant stung her.

"Little friends," she said. "You kept me company in the Tower and now you have protected me here."

But she couldn't stay in the forest, in case the knights returned. "If I can find Hans," she thought, "I can hide in his palace."

At the gates of Hans' palace, a guard with arms the size of fire logs blocked her way. He eyed her as if she was something he'd just picked off his boot. "Are you Lady Olga's maid?" he demanded.

Elisa had no idea who Lady Olga was, but it seemed a good way of getting inside. "Yes," she replied, "that's me."

"Come with me," the guard barked.

Elisa couldn't spot Hans anywhere, as the guard led her across a courtyard and through a banqueting hall, to a room where a noble lady was being dressed.

"Your new maid, Lady Olga," the guard announced, with a grunt.

"About time too!" Lady Olga snapped. "Well,

don't just stand there, girl! Help me prepare for tomorrow's wedding."

Elisa was so confused, all she could reply was, "What wedding?"

"My wedding of course! To Prince Hans."

Elisa did her best not to look shocked, as her heart broke into a million pieces. Her beloved Hans was getting married! That night, after she had polished Lady Olga's shoes, Elisa sat watching servants decorate the courtyard for the wedding ceremony. She sighed long and hard.

"What a fool I was to think that Hans would still love me."

From where she sat she could see to the forest, at the edge of the kingdom. Its trees, silhouetted against the moon, swayed gently, as if to beckon her back. Tomorrow, she decided, she would return and live among the trees, and the nettles – her only friends.

The next morning, as sunlight began to trickle through the tall palace windows, Elisa crept through the banqueting hall... But, once again, the grumpy guard blocked her path.

"Come with me," he growled.

He didn't say "or else" but he sounded as if he meant "or else," so Elisa followed him to Lady Olga's bathroom.

Several servants were struggling to open the door. One of them swung a hammer at the handle, while another cried, "STAND BACK!" and charged at the door like a battering ram, but all he did was hurt his arm.

"What's going on?" Elisa asked.

"The key broke in the lock," the guard grunted. "Lady Olga is trapped inside."

Elisa didn't understand what any of this had to do with her. *She* certainly wasn't going to charge at the door.

"Is that my new maid?" Lady Olga cried.

"Yes, my lady," Elisa replied.

"Listen to me, girl. My wedding is in half an hour. Many important people have come a very long way to see me be married. I cannot tell them I am locked in a bathroom! I would die of shame. The wedding must go ahead as planned, with or without me."

"Without you, my lady?"

"You shall take my place," Lady Olga yelled.

"We are the same size, so if you wear a veil no one will know it's not me. Then, once the locksmith has freed me, I will secretly take my place again at the ceremony."

Elisa burst out laughing. There was no way she was going to pretend to be...

Lady Olga's servants pounced. Grabbing and pushing, they dressed Elisa in a wedding dress and veil, and thrust her out into the courtyard.

Trumpets blared and the wedding guests cheered, as they saw the bride. A servant scattered rose petals from Elisa to an altar at the front of the courtyard.

"They're all crazy," Elisa muttered.

She was about to make a dash for the palace gates, when a golden carriage rattled through the entrance. Elisa watched as the carriage door opened – and out stepped Prince Hans.

Elisa barely recognized him. He looked stiff and formal in royal clothes, as if he had a wooden plank down the back of his velvet tunic. His face was different too. The sparkle was gone from his eyes and, even though he waved to the guests, there was no trace of a smile on his face.

Elisa held her hands behind her back to hide their tremble.

"Lady Olga," Hans said, dryly. "My father says we must be married."

Oh Hans, Elisa thought, as the trumpets grew louder and he led the way to the altar. Suddenly, she cried out. "STOP!"

The trumpets fell silent and the guests gasped. Elisa yanked Hans back so hard that he almost tumbled over. She had spotted something on the

*Elisa didn't notice, but Hans stood staring
at her as if he had seen a ghost.*

ground near the altar – a nettle that Hans had been about to step on. She crouched and stroked its fragile leaves. "Little friend," she whispered, "you are safe now."

Elisa didn't notice, but Hans stood staring at her as if he had seen a ghost.

The wedding ceremony was long and boring, and throughout it Hans kept gazing at his bride with the same look of confusion and fear. Scared her voice might give her away, Elisa barely said another word, even as Hans led her from the courtyard to the banqueting hall.

By then, Lady Olga was free. When Hans wasn't looking, she dragged Elisa into a side room. "Give me back my dress!" she snapped. "And be gone!"

A minute later, Lady Olga sat beside her new husband at the wedding feast. Hans looked even more baffled as she removed her veil and planted a sloppy kiss on his cheek.

Elisa watched from the side room. She saw

Hans lean over to his new bride and whisper in her ear, and the last pieces of her heart crumbled to dust. As she fled, she swore she would never set foot in another palace.

Later that day, Elisa sat alone in the forest, watching birds flutter and bees buzz and nettles sway in the breeze. She knew she would stay there for the rest of her life, but none of it seemed the same without Hans. "Oh nettles," she sighed, "why did he have to get married?"

"Because I'm not as brave as you," a familiar voice replied.

Elisa leaped up, as a figure stepped from behind the trees. She staggered back, hiding behind some nettles for fear that she'd been caught by one of the palace guards. But when the voice spoke again, she knew it was no enemy.

Hans stepped closer. "Elisa," he said, "I do not need to see your face to know it is you. But I was told that you were dead."

"Who told you such lies?" Elisa demanded, edging out of hiding.

"My father," Hans replied.

"Did he also tell you to marry Lady Olga?"

Elisa felt bad. She hadn't meant to snap, and now Hans hung his head in shame.

"I could not refuse," he groaned. "My father is the king."

"But he is not *our* king," Elisa said, "and neither is my father. They never were. This forest was our kingdom, remember?"

"I remember," Hans said. "I wish I had been as strong as you."

Elisa sighed, and sat on a fallen tree trunk. She was happy to see Hans, but there was so much she didn't understand. "Did you know it was me at the wedding?" she asked.

"No," Hans replied. "But when I saw you talk to that nettle, I thought of you. At the feast, I asked Lady Olga why she spoke to the plant. She told me she hadn't, and that it was ridiculous to talk to a plant. I knew then that she wasn't the one who had stood by me at the altar. There is only one person who speaks to nettles. When I realized you were gone, I thought I might find you here."

"There is no other place for me," Elisa explained. "But... why are you here?"

Hans' face lit up with a grin and he skipped up to her. "I ran away," he said. "I'm never going back to that palace."

Elisa laughed. She dearly loved Hans, but sometimes he was a little ridiculous. "Hans,"

she said, "have you forgotten so quickly?
You only just got married."

"No, I didn't forget. How can I be
married to Lady Olga if she wasn't with
me at the altar?"

Elisa hadn't thought of that.
Hans was right – he
wasn't married at all.

"I know now
that there is only
one person I
could ever marry,"
Hans added.

He sank to one knee
in front of Elisa. "Elisa, will you do
me the privilege of– "

Elisa burst out laughing again.

"Oh Hans," she interrupted. "If you ask me to
marry you I will scream so loudly that every knight
in the two kingdoms will know where we are."

"Ah," Hans muttered. His cheeks flushed pink

with embarrassment. "So do you not want to marry me then?"

"Hans," Elisa explained, "this morning you thought I was dead, this afternoon you tried to marry someone else, and *now* you want to marry me? Maybe we should just forget about weddings for now? Besides, who here *could* marry us?"

Hans' cheeks turned an even brighter pink. He hadn't really thought about that. He turned, gazing around the glade. He saw squirrels playing in branches, bees buzzing at a hive, and nettles swaying in a breeze. This forest sat between the two kingdoms, but it felt so far from all of their squabbles. More than ever, he wanted to stay.

"Well," Hans said. "Perhaps I could live with you here?"

Elisa looked at him, as sunlight fell through the trees, and her eyes sparkled like diamonds.

"Perhaps you could," she said, with a smile.

They did live together in the forest, where they built a small house and grew things to eat, and were never again told to act like royalty. They walked among the birds and the bees and the nettles and the trees. Whenever they heard the clash and clatter of swords, or cries of knights fighting on the nearby hill, Elisa and Hans paused whatever they were doing, to look at one another and smile.

This fairy tale is based on a very old English story. The same story inspired the famous playwright, William Shakespeare, when he wrote his play 'King Lear'.

The Wise Princess

There was once an old king who lived with his three daughters in a crumbling castle. Although he was old, he was not always wise, and he had a weakness for fine words and flattery.

One day, for want of any other amusements, he decided to set his daughters a test.

"Tell me how much you love me, my dear daughters," he said. "And I will give you rewards to match your words."

The eldest princess answered at once.

"Dear Father, I love you as much as all the world," she announced proudly.

The king was well pleased, and gave her a necklace of emeralds, as green as the lands that he ruled.

Then the middle princess spoke up.

"Dearest Father, I love you as much as life itself," she said prettily.

The king was delighted, and gave her a necklace of rubies, as red as heart's blood.

Then it was the turn of the youngest, Greta. The king turned to her and smiled, expecting more glittering praise. He patted his pocket, where a necklace of starry diamonds awaited.

Greta thought for a long time before she spoke. She wanted to be sure that she had found exactly the right words.

"My Father," she said at last. "I love you as much as salt."

The king forgot the necklace and stared at her in surprise. "Salt?" he repeated, disbelieving.

Greta returned his gaze, undaunted. She knew she had spoken the truth. "Yes, salt."

The king leaned forward. "Salt is for cooks, not kings," he warned, jabbing a finger in the air. "Speak again!"

Greta shook her head, tongue-tied by her father's reaction.

Her silence made the king explode with anger.

"You are not worthy to be a king's daughter," he thundered. "Get out! And don't come back!"

Cheeks burning, Greta fled.

She ran from the castle, past fields and pastures and woods, into the wild lands beyond. Salty tears stung her face. She ran until she could run no more, and then she sank down to rest.

Beside her, rushes nodded and waved on the shores of a lake. Greta scooped up a handful of cool water and splashed her face. Then she looked around, wondering what to do next. She had never been so far from home alone before.

"I can't go back, so I must go on," she told herself, trying to feel brave. "But where?"

A sudden gust of wind blew up, sending ripples racing across the lake. Greta shivered. Her fine silk gown was no protection against the weather.

"Brrr... I wish I had a cloak," she thought, watching the rushes rustle and sway in the wind. That gave her an idea. She picked an armful of rush leaves and stems, and set to work.

Patiently she braided and wove, and wove and braided... until at last, as the sun sank, she finished and held up what she had made: a long cloak with a stiff, pointed hood, made entirely of rushes.

By now, her fingers were numb with cold. Quickly, she pulled on the cloak. It was rough and prickly, unlike anything she had worn before, but it felt warm. She glanced at her reflection in the lake. With the cloak clutched around her, her fine clothes were well hidden. She looked like any poor country servant.

That gave her another idea. "If I look like a servant, perhaps I can work as one."

A little way off, she knew, stood a large manor house. An old lord, a friend of her father's, lived there. "I'll see if I can get work in his kitchen," she decided. "I've always liked watching the cooks in the castle kitchens."

Tap, tap, tappity-tap!

Greta knocked nervously on the back door of the manor house. After a pause, it banged open to reveal a grumpy-looking housekeeper.

"Yes? What do you want?" she snapped frostily.

"Please, ma'am, have you any work for a kitchen maid?" asked Greta politely.

"We-e-ell..." said the housekeeper, hesitating to take on someone so peculiarly dressed. She stared at Greta's cloak and tutted. "I suppose we DO need someone to do the washing up," she admitted at last. She waved one hand at a huge mountain of greasy, grimy pots and pans, flanked by towers of gravy-stained plates, teetering beside the sink.

Greta's heart sank slightly, but she stepped inside, pushed up her sleeves and set to work. She rubbed and scrubbed and scoured, until the pots sparkled and her arms ached.

Meanwhile, the housekeeper got on with the cooking. Unfortunately, she wasn't very good at it. Greta tried not to wince as she saw her drown delicate dishes in mustard, burn the bread and curdle the cream.

"I'm not even sure WHAT that's supposed to be," she thought, as yet another unappetizing platter was carried past, followed by a whiff of rotten turnips.

After dinner, the lord went straight to bed, looking faintly green.

The next morning, the lord did not come down for breakfast.

"He's sick," said the servants. "He says he doesn't want any food."

The lord did not come down for lunch either. Instead, the housekeeper sent up a tray of food.

Urgh! thought Greta, catching a glimpse. Not surprisingly, the tray came back untouched.

"What shall we do?" sighed the housekeeper. "He's too sick even to eat."

Greta thought she might be able to help. Shyly, she asked: "Please, may I cook something?"

"Please yourself," said the housekeeper, with a shrug. "I've tried everything I know."

So Greta washed her hands and tied on an apron, and rummaged through the pantry for fresh ingredients. Then she began to slice, dice, simmer and stir... Before long, a new smell crept through the kitchen. The other servants sniffed appreciatively and smiled.

Greta had made a mouth-watering broth.

A servant carried a bowlful up to the lord – and this time, he did not refuse it.

"Mmm, delicious!" he croaked.

The lord asked for another bowlful, and another... and, at last, he began to get better.

When the lord was up and about again, he summoned the housekeeper.

"Who made that delicious broth for me while I was sick?" he asked.

"Well, er, um... I did," claimed the housekeeper, unwilling to admit she had let another servant cook for her master. But the lie made her blush as bright as a beetroot.

"Aha," said the lord, who was no fool. "Then please can you tell me the recipe?"

The housekeeper hesitated. In truth, she hadn't the faintest idea how Greta had made the broth. "I, um, er... I'd need to check with the maid," she stammered eventually.

"Aha," said the lord again, nodding thoughtfully. "Will you send this maid to see me? Thank you."

Greta tidied her hair and smoothed down her clothes, and went to see the lord. She made sure to wear her cloak too, worried that he might recognize her without it.

She found him sitting by the fire, looking almost his old self again. He didn't have a clue that this maid with her rough rush cloak and a smudge of flour on her nose was his old friend's daughter. But he did tell her that he liked her broth so much, he wanted her to become his head cook.

Greta's face lit up and she agreed readily. "It'll be much nicer to cook instead of washing up all day!" she thought to herself happily. "I just hope the housekeeper won't mind..."

To Greta's relief, when the housekeeper found out, she was pleased too. "Now I can concentrate on the housekeeping," she said, with a sigh of relief. "I never liked cooking anyway."

So Greta became a cook – and a very talented cook at that. With her in charge of the kitchen, whether it was breakfast, lunch or dinner, every dish was a delight... and everyone in the manor house grew plump and happy.

The lord was so impressed by it all that he decided to hold a banquet – something he had not done for years – in order for his friends to come and taste Greta's cooking too.

"Guess what," the housekeeper told Greta excitedly when she found out. "He even sent an invitation to the king himself – and the king has accepted!"

"The king?" Greta smiled a small, secret smile.

"You know, that gives me an idea…"

On the day of the banquet, Greta rose before dawn. She sliced and seared and sizzled and stirred. She baked enormous golden pies and tiny, buttery tarts. She simmered rich soups and stews. She built up tottering towers of cream cakes, studded with candied fruits and sugared flowers. She was determined that this would be a feast fit for a king.

Every dish she made, she seasoned herself.

"Bring me all the salt cellars," she told the startled housekeeper. "I don't want there to be any confusion. Everything today must be just right… especially the seasoning!"

Delicious smells wafted from the kitchen, while in the rest of the manor house servants scurried busily to and fro, polishing the silver, lighting candles and setting the table in the great hall. Banners hung from the walls and goblets glittered… until, at last, everything was ready.

A fanfare of trumpets announced the arrival of

"Bring me all the salt cellars," she told the startled housekeeper.

the king. Greta watched from the shadows like
any poor servant, disguised in her cloak of rushes,
as the lord led the king to a chair at the very head
of the table.

The lord clapped his hands together loudly,
then called out in the silence that followed. "Let
the banquet begin!"

The first dish was a steaming silver tureen of
soup. A solemn-faced butler ladled out delicate

bowlfuls, and set the first one in front of the king.
Carefully, he lifted his spoon and took a single sip.
Then he frowned and put the spoon down again.

"How odd," he said. "It has no taste."

The lord tried his own bowl and shook his head.

"Pass the salt!" he demanded. But strangely,
there was none on the table – and none to be found
in the kitchen or the pantry or any of the store
rooms either.

"Never mind," snapped the lord impatiently. "Hurry up and bring the next dish!"

Two footmen stepped forward at once with another tureen, this time brimming with stew. The butler served it up onto silver plates and again set the first one in front of the king.

The king picked up his fork and took a nibble. Then he shook his head sadly.

"This is just as tasteless," he sighed.

The lord tried it. "Ugh – what's going on? This needs salt as well!"

The same thing happened with the next dish... and the next... and the next... Each one looked incredible, but tasted of nothing. The pastries were entirely plain and the pies could have been stuffed with old socks, for all that anyone could taste of them. Even the bread was just so much fluff.

"I am SO sorry, Your Highness," stammered the lord, hot with embarrassment as yet another failed dish was carried away. "I don't know what's happened to my cook."

The king shook his head. "Please, there is no
need to apologize. In fact this has been a wonderful
meal, for it has taught me something important."
His voice cracked, and he
paused for a moment to
rub his eyes before
continuing. "I only
wish my youngest
daughter was
here, so that I
could tell her..."
His voice trailed
off, leaving the
room in silence.

At that moment,
Greta stepped forward,
pulled off the tattered rush
cloak which had concealed her fine dress for so
long, and looked boldly up at the king.

"Here I am, Father," she said, in a soft, clear
voice, looking and sounding every inch a princess

again. The lord gaped in amazement.

The king looked up. Eyes glistening, he held out his arms. Greta stepped into them and they embraced at last.

"My darling daughter, I have missed you so much these past weeks! I am sorry I sent you away. Please can you forgive me?" he begged. "I was foolish and proud, and did not understand the words you spoke. Now I realize you were wiser than I knew. Truly, a love like salt is the most precious of all – for without it, everything is dull and without taste!"

Greta nodded and smiled. She could hardly speak for happiness, but this time she did not need any words. Her smile was all the king needed to know he was forgiven.

Then Greta told everyone where she had hidden the salt cellars, and the housekeeper ran to fetch them, while she and her father sat down happily side by side, to eat and talk and laugh together once more.

And when the food was finally served a second time, sprinkled with salt and seasoned with love, everyone thought it was the best meal they had ever tasted.

This fairy tale is based on the story
'Tam Lin' which was originally sung as a
ballad. It has been sung on the Scottish
Borders for over 500 years.

Fearless Fiona
and the
Spellbound
Knight

If you were to travel on the lonely road between Selkirk and Newark Castle you might notice several odd things about the enchanted forest of Caterhaugh, which lurks between them.

For one, even during the winter months, the oaks are still covered in spring-green leaves. For another, the weather is often quite different inside the forest and out.

In summer, while the warm sun blazes down
on the moors and meadows, a chill mist cloaks the
trees. When autumn gales thrash the country for
miles around, the forest stands still and calm as
the dead.

But it is not on account of its strange weather
that locals shun the place. It is the fact that some
visitors to Caterhaugh never come out. Every
family in Selkirk has forbidden their children
from ever entering the woods. The few, brave
woodcutters who dare to venture inside keep to
the paths, and are careful only to collect fallen
branches. They would not cut down a living tree
for any price, and they know to avoid the well at
the heart of the forest at all costs.

But still... there is something... tempting about
the deep, green silence of the forest. Lovely, richly
scented flowers flourish in lush clumps about the
roots of the trees. As far as anyone from Selkirk
knows, they grow nowhere else. Fruit, nuts, acorns
and mushrooms are abundant in their season.

The paths are well swept and inviting. It is almost as if someone – or something – wanted you to take a walk beneath the branches...

"I wonder what would actually happen if I went in there," thought Fiona as she headed home from her grandmother's house.

She always thought the same thing. Ever since she was a little girl, she'd thought it each time she had to take the long track that wound cautiously around the edge of the forest. Her parents had always insisted she made this long, unnecessary detour. The forest was too dangerous, they said. She must never go in.

A little voice popped into her mind, unbidden. Really, why should it always be a two-hour round trip

to deliver eggs to her grandmother?

"What's the worst that could happen, eh Lupin?" Fiona glanced at the dog who was trotting beside her. "The woodcutters go in there all the time, don't they? It's only a wee wood. I'd be straight through in ten minutes easy, and then you'd get your dinner sooner. You'd like that, wouldn't you?"

Lupin ignored her and carried on down the track. From the set of his shoulders, it was quite clear what this dog felt about that forest: keep away!

Fiona always tried to be a good, dutiful daughter. Normally, she would have shrugged and followed her dog. But this time, she didn't. She couldn't have told you why she didn't, but there it was. Instead, she took a step towards the trees. And then another.

She put down her empty basket and did not look back. Lupin glanced nervously at the forest, and whined.

"You run on then, worry-wart," said Fiona. "I'll see you on the other side."

Another step. Now she felt the forest reaching out to embrace her. One more step and the branches would be overhead. Still, Fiona was not afraid. An odd calm had settled over her mind, smoothing everything, like mist on the moor.

Lupin was a brave dog. He darted forward once, twice and even a third time. Each time he stopped dead, two strides short of Fiona. It looked funny, as if he'd hit an invisible wall. Forlorn, he put his tail between his legs and whined, pacing back and forth. He would not come closer.

"Silly dog," said Fiona. "What is there to be scared of? It's just trees."

She took another step and the branches closed in. Blithely, uncaring, Fiona walked on into the forest.

Soon she'd forgotten all about Lupin, her basket and even her mother and father, waiting for her at home.

How could she remember anything when

everything she saw was so beautiful? It was an elusive beauty, hovering at the corner of her vision. There was a shimmer in the air – a little wobble of rainbow that seemed to wrap her up and make everything delightful. For a time, Fiona just stood there, waving her hands through the air, watching the rainbows flow from them like ribbons.

"Golly," giggled Fiona. "Shall we see what else there is to see?"

She carried on into the woods. She had a strong sense that she must go deeper. She could feel it tugging at her bones, leading her on, and even though she couldn't say why she chose the paths that she was choosing, she knew they were the right ones.

"On we go," she sang to herself. Her long skirt swished around her legs as she skipped along, getting faster.

She passed a clearing filled with slender bushes that had grown so they looked just like frozen people. They had arms and legs, heads, hands and

feet. Most strangely of all, when she passed her
fingers in front of her face and stirred the rainbows
in the air, the bushes seemed to move.

Now they were all looking at her.

Fiona carried on, deeper and deeper into the
woods. Some time passed. How long she could not
say. So many intriguing sights and sounds – a tree
covered in every kind of fruit, a soft smile made

out of shadows, a stream of swirling music – but she did not pause, or dawdle or stop for even one moment until she was standing in the place where she felt she was meant to be.

"Here at last." Fiona gave a deep, satisfied sigh. She had arrived in a neat little grove at the heart of the forest. In the middle of the grove was an old well. A rose bush grew in a tangle over its ancient stones. Its flowers were by far the most beautiful things that Fiona had ever seen. They were a rich, deep red, darker than blood.

She wanted a rose. How could she not? And the bush had no thorns. It would be so easy to pick one.

She reached out, and broke a stem.

SNAP!

Everything changed.

A knight was suddenly standing beside the well. He was tall and thin. A long sword hung from his belt. The green chain mail that covered him from

Everything changed.
A knight was suddenly standing beside the well.

head to foot seemed to be made out of twisted vines. Bright flowers grew from his helmet and covered his shield.

The spell that had gripped hold of Fiona had snapped with the stem. She realized all at once where she was, and what she'd done.

"The fairy forest is too dangerous. You must never go in." She could remember her mother saying precisely those words to her this very morning. The warning was so familiar, Fiona had not even noticed the words as they were spoken, though she could hear them very clearly now.

And here she was, all the same.

"You're a fool, Fiona Kirkbride," she snapped. Her anger at her own stupidity blazed white hot. "Lupin knew you were wrong! But did you listen to him? No, so here you are, with a blooming fairy popping out of a well!"

The knight looked a little perplexed at her outburst. He held out his hand.

"Lady, you must come with me..." His words

sounded thick and strange, as if the knight was remembering the language, or maybe how to move his tongue.

Fiona turned her fury on him. "Must I indeed? And why, you great lump? Because you say so?"

The fairy knight didn't move his hand. "You took the rose."

"And what of that?"

"There are rules. That rose belongs to my noble queen."

"Rules get broken. I broke my parents' rules to come here. So now I will break your noble queen's. Just watch."

Fiona's mind was completely clear now. She knew she had to run. Buying time by tidying her hair – which had become a little messy in her wander through the enchanted forest – she looked about the grove for a way to escape. But something was very wrong. She could not see the path that she had come in by, nor any path at all. Only a wall of trees and thorns, blocking her way.

She had seen no thorns on the way in.

"Lady, come with me to the Pleasant Land," said the knight. "Do not be afraid. It is truly a beautiful place."

"No!" Fiona snarled her defiance. "I will not."

The knight made a grab for her. Fiona jumped away, but he was much too fast and closed the gap in a blink. He grabbed her by the arm.

"You brute! You bully!" cried Fiona, pulling away. His fingers were cold and his grip was iron strong. "Just who do you think you are?"

To her surprise, the knight shivered, and let go of her arm.

"I... I..." he stammered. His hand dropped to his side.

This reaction was so strange and unexpected that, for a moment, Fiona was stunned, and stood there gaping too – but she recovered her wits quickly enough to seize her opportunity.

"You will not answer me?" asked Fiona. "Is that it? How odd. Well! I will certainly not go gallivanting off with some haughty fellow who won't even introduce himself. Tell me, what is your name, fairy?"

Again, the knight shook, as if he'd been struck. He stood quite still. Fiona knew she should have been scared, but she wasn't. Somehow, she was winning this fight.

Now it was her turn to take a step towards the knight.

"What is your name?" said Fiona again. "I'll tell you my name, but only if you'll tell me yours."

Still, the knight didn't answer. Instead, he quivered.

Fiona reached out and snapped up the visor on the fairy knight's helmet. It made a satisfying click.

"Oh."

Fiona had never met a fairy before, but even so, the face beneath the helmet was surprising. It was not some proud, thin-lipped elf king from her grandmother's tales. Nor was it a hairy monster with teeth like daggers. It was just a boy, hardly older than herself.

He had dark hair and a pleasant face. Only his eyes were strange, misted with empty clouds like a thick sea fog.

Often, the ballads that Fiona had heard sung around the hearth on a long winter's evening had told tales of fairies, and true love at first sight. Fiona, being a sensible, practical girl had scoffed at both. But now, trapped in a fairy forest, it was easy to believe in one, so why not the other?

Fiona felt something stir in her heart. She took the knight's hand in hers even though it was cold. "My name is Fiona," she whispered.

For the second time that day, a spell was broken. The boy blinked and when his eyes

opened, they had
cleared. She saw
they were blue like
a summer sky.

"My name is Tam
Lin." He smiled.
"How did you know?"

"How did I know what?" Fiona grinned back.
They were both delighted with each other.

"How to break my enchantment."

"I don't know, Tam Lin," said Fiona. "It just
seemed the right thing to do."

Again, they looked each other over, a little shyly
maybe, but quite comfortable with the silence and
each other – that is until Tam Lin remembered
where they were. He frowned at the well, as if
someone might be watching.

"I am very grateful to you, Fiona," he said. "But
you must leave now. It is not safe. I can show you
the way. Come." He waved his hand and an arch
opened up in the wall of trees and brambles.

"But will you not be leaving yourself?" Fiona felt her heart's contentment shatter into pieces. It was funny how quickly things could change. She didn't want to leave him at all.

Tam Lin shook his head. "I am bound to the queen. I can never leave."

"But you're not a fairy," said Fiona. "You're a boy. Don't you want to come with me?"

"I wish with all my heart that I might," said Tam Lin, and Fiona, looking in his eyes, could see that this was true. "But the queen caught me and I went with her beneath the green hill. I ate her food and drank the water and now I can never go back. But you can. You must. Come." He pulled her quickly through the arch and into the forest.

This time, Fiona took his hand gladly. It felt hot now, where before it had been cold as ice. But the forest did not seem as lovely as before. Clumsy, bushy figures stalked slowly towards them with grasping, branchy fingers. The shadows had teeth.

They ran.

Fearless Fiona

"I will not leave without you," Fiona gasped, gripping his hand fiercely.

"You will," said Tam Lin. "You must."

"There must be something I can do."

For a brief instant, Tam Lin hesitated. "No," he said. "There isn't."

Fiona knew at once that he was lying. "Tell me," she said. "And I will do it."

Again, Tam Lin hesitated.

Ahead, Fiona saw the edge of the forest and her basket and her dog, Lupin, whom she had so easily forgotten.

Behind them, they both heard the baying of an
unearthly hound. It had the triumphant, frantic
whine of a dog that had picked up a scent. The
sound froze Fiona's blood.

"Tell me," said Fiona fiercely. "Quickly. There is
no time."

"Once a year, at midnight, on All Hallows' Eve,"
began Tam Lin, as the baying of the hound grew
louder still, "the fairy queen leads out her knights
in a great parade. They say..." And now again, he
hesitated and looked at Fiona as if he did not dare
say any more.

"What?" said Fiona, trying to remain calm,
because the hounds, and there was more than
one hound now, seemed ever closer. "What do
they say?"

"They say..." Tam Lin blushed. "They say that
they who would their true love win, must wait at
Miles Cross and grab him right off his horse. And
hold on, no matter what. Hold on tight, until it is
too hot to bear, then throw him in the well...

And now you must run! Go!"

He shoved Fiona out into the sunshine.

She stumbled, and fell down on the grass.
A dog was all over her. For an instant, Fiona was
terrified, but then she realized that it was just
Lupin, licking her face and
wagging his tail and
barking ecstatically
all at once. By
the time Fiona
had disentangled
herself from him
and looked back into
the forest, Tam Lin and
the fairy hounds were gone.

She returned home in a daze, and she might
have believed that it was all just a dream – if she
did not still have the blood-red rose in her hand.

That night, and every night thereafter, Fiona
dreamed of the fairy knight with the boy's sweet
face. She counted down the days to All Hallows'

Eve. There was never a question in her mind about
what she would do – though she did wish that Tam
Lin had been a little clearer in his instructions. She
had so many questions.

What had he meant about things getting too
hot? And why did she have to throw him in a well?

Fiona kept the rose hidden in her room and
looked at it every night. It did not fade or lose its
bloom. Her parents knew that something was not
right, and asked many times what troubled her, but
she gave them no good answer. On All Hallows'
Eve she kissed her family goodnight with a fierce
tenderness, knowing that it might be the last time
she did.

"You're a good girl, Fiona," murmured her
mother sleepily.

"I love you, Ma," said Fiona.

When the house was asleep, she slipped out
in secret and – shrugging on her cape – walked
quickly across the misty moor. She left Lupin
behind, though his company would have been

welcome on such a ghostly, gloomy night.

Miles Cross was a lonely crossroads, far from any light. There was no moon. Fiona crouched down behind a clump of gorse and shivered in the eerie dark. She listened to the wind moaning through the heather. By her reckoning, it must be midnight soon.

She did not have long to wait.

The first sign of the parade's approach was a faint silvery jingle-jangle – the ringing of fairy bridles. The second was the soft clip-clop of unshod hooves, for no fairy horse wears iron.

A moment later, a long train of horsemen carrying shining shields and long-plumed lances came trotting over the brow of the hill and clattered through Miles Cross. Although there was no moon, Fiona could see each of the fairy knights quite clearly. The air bent and sparkled around them, as if a sun was shining on them in another world.

They would have been beautiful, if not for their

faces. Their expressions were proud and cold, and their eyes glittered with pale fire.

Fiona, hardly daring to breathe, searched each deathly face for Tam Lin, but she did not find it. She saw the end of the column approaching, and began to worry that she had missed him – or worse, that he had not ridden out with the other knights.

The fairy queen rode last of all. Her horse breathed flames and struck lightning from the

ground with its hooves. Her dress was as black as night, and glittered with a thousand stars. Her face was as beautiful and distant as the moon.

Beside her, a handsome young knight rode on a milk-white steed. From afar, Fiona recognized his flower-covered shield.

"Tam Lin!" she breathed.

Her heart was hammering in her chest. Slowly, the queen and her companion rode closer.

Fiona waited, tensed and ready.

Just as the pair rode by, she jumped out from her hiding place. She grabbed hold of Tam Lin's leg and dragged him from the saddle of his horse. Mindful of his warning, she held on to the knight as tightly as she could.

The fairy riders formed a circle around her. They did not say a word, but the queen pointed her clawed finger at Fiona, screaming a terrible curse in a language Fiona did not understand.

Beneath Fiona's hands, Tam Lin's body shaped and shifted. It shrank down and in on itself, writhing and coiling.

"Hold on, hold on!" cried Fiona.

Writhing within her fingers, Tam Lin had become an adder. His arrow-shaped head bit and hissed, but Fiona gripped him by the neck and held on still. She was terribly afraid.

"My love, my love, I will not let you go," she whispered as if the words were a charm that might protect her.

With a snort of fury, the queen raised her finger and cursed the knight again.

And now his sinuous body began to grow and flex. Muscles rippled and stretched. Fiona was lifted up high in the air as Tam Lin became a great brown bear.

He raised his shaggy head and roared defiance. Fiona, gripping on to his neck, was tossed this way and that. She dug her fingers into his thick coat and held on for her life.

"My love, my love," whispered Fiona again. "I will not let you go."

Once more, the fairy queen hissed with rage. With her ice-cold finger she drew an awful symbol in the air.

As Tam Lin began to warp again, his bellow became a savage snarl. His teeth gleamed white in the dark and grew longer than kitchen knives. His tail thrashed and his sharp claws tried to tear poor Fiona from his back.

But though Fiona had never seen a lion before,

she was wise enough
to see that a lion's
mane makes for
a tidy grip –
and for all that
the king of
beasts tried to
shake her free,
she clung on still.
"My love, my
love," whispered Fiona
again. "I will not let you go."

The fury of the fairy queen burned brighter
than the sun. Her mask of beauty fell away, and
her true soul shone through: warped and ugly and
filled with spite.

She screamed a black curse that tore the air and
ripped the earth and set the world spinning with
its power.

The lion shrank away to nothing, but in its
place Fiona felt a terrible, burning heat. A hot coal

blazed in her hands. It scorched her fingers raw.

But now brave Fiona remembered what Tam Lin had said: "Hold on tight, until it is too hot to bear," and she understood.

Despite the blistering heat from the red-hot coal she held on tight, and stumbled to the well. No fairy made a move to stop her.

She waited until she could not stand the burning any longer.

"Be free, Tam Lin!" she cried and threw the blazing coal down into the darkness.

Time seemed to hang still as the brave little glow plummeted down the shaft, illuminating the dark.

"My love, my love," whispered Fiona.

The moment the spark hit the water, it hissed and died. In the darkness, Fiona was sure she had failed.

Then a roaring light was all about her, and a warm hand grabbed her own. The agonizing pain in her fingers vanished like a dream.

"You're a brave girl, Fiona," said Tam Lin. He was standing beside her dressed in ordinary clothes, as if they'd just stepped out for a stroll.

He was quite as handsome as before.

The queen of the fairies was crying tears of rage. "I should have ripped out your eyes, girl," she hissed, "and trapped you in a tree. For now, my Tam Lin is lost to me."

Fiona smiled at the queen. She knew that she had no power over her.

"I don't think it pays for your kind to be out at sunrise, my lady," she answered. "Shouldn't you be on your way?"

She spoke with a spark in her eye, defiance in her voice and her head held proud and high, as brave as you like. The queen saw at once how it was – and gave a silvery laugh, for a fairy's mood is as changeable as spring sun.

"You are a fine one, girl. My Tam Lin is yours now. Treat him well, or we will surely meet again."

And she whistled to her riders, and the fairies

galloped away into the night.

Again, Tam Lin and Fiona looked at each other, a little shyly maybe, but quite comfortable with the silence and each other.

"Come," said Fiona at last, holding out her hand. "Let's go home, Tam Lin. It's quite a walk."

Joyfully, they walked back across the moor. They arrived home as dawn's purple fingers were creeping over the heather-covered hills.

"I hope you like porridge," said Fiona. "We'll be just in time for breakfast."

Forgotten Fairy Tales

Edited by Lesley Sims
Designed by Sam Whibley
Managing designer: Russell Punter
Digital design: Nick Wakeford